Darling Remy,

Do you remember the early years, my love, when we first opened the Hotel Marchand? We were so busy chasing after our dream of creating a world-class hotel for visitors to our beautiful city of New Orleans. While you were working your magic in the kitchen, building up a restaurant that would put Cajun cooking on the map, I was scouring estate sales searching for just the right pieces to make our guests feel as if they had stepped back in time. And all the while our daughters just kept coming. We had fun, Remy, because we had each other and our dream.

I think of those days often, now that the hotel is having so many problems. I console myself by remembering that we made it through those tough times. There is a wonderful jazz singer at the hotel. Her name is Holly Carlyle, and when I hear her sing her beautiful songs of love, I know that even though you are no longer beside me, your spirit is with me, making me confident that the hotel we built together will always survive.

All my love,
Anne

Dear Reader,

Writing a book set in the city of New Orleans was a pleasure. The city itself has a personality and a character that you won't find anywhere else in the world. Walking down narrow streets and looking up at bright splashes of flowers tumbling from window boxes, you can almost pretend you've taken a step back in time. Until, that is, you hear the jazz streaming from the clubs that crowd the French Quarter.

In the aftermath of Hurricane Katrina, the city itself was battered, but the people who make up that amazing city are undefeatable. In this series, I believe we're honoring New Orleans and its citizens and I hope you enjoy my little corner of the Hotel Marchand.

Love,

Maureen

MAUREEN CHILD

Bourbon Street Blues

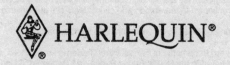

HARLEQUIN®

TORONTO • NEW YORK • LONDON
AMSTERDAM • PARIS • SYDNEY • HAMBURG
STOCKHOLM • ATHENS • TOKYO • MILAN • MADRID
PRAGUE • WARSAW • BUDAPEST • AUCKLAND

ISBN-13: 978-0-373-38942-1
ISBN-10:   0-373-38942-6

BOURBON STREET BLUES

Copyright © 2006 by Harlequin Books S.A.

Maureen Child is acknowledged as the author of this work.

www.eHarlequin.com

Printed in U.S.A.

Maureen Child is a native Californian, still waiting for a change of seasons. As the author of over ninety novels, she's written under several pseudonyms and many different genres from historical to paranormal to contemporary romance. Maureen loves a happy ending and when she isn't writing, she's reading or traveling with her husband.

CHAPTER ONE

HOLLY CARLYLE GAVE HER accompanist a grin and leaned across the gleaming black surface of the piano top. Swinging her long, auburn hair back away from her face, she tapped out an echo of the song that had just ended with the tips of her red-polished fingernails. "Tommy, that was *fabulous,*" she said. "If we can keep it together that tightly tonight, we're so gonna rock this place."

Tommy Hayes winced as his long, mocha-colored fingers slid along the piano keys, sending a *chirrru-upp* of sound into the still air. "*Jazz* the place, Holly," he said, shaking his head. "We don't rock, we *jazz...*."

She laughed, straightened and stacked the sheets of music together neatly. "Yeah, but when our jazz is smoking, we really rock."

Tommy sighed and stroked the keys gently, as he would a lover's body. The overhead lights shone down on his dark hair, liberally laced with gray. He wore two silver rings on each hand and his black suit hung on his lean body. Tommy swore he'd been playing jazz piano in New Orleans since God was a boy. And nobody played it better.

Holly had been working with him for nearly fourteen years and she'd never been happier. The older man had become almost a father to her—something Holly relished since she'd been on her own most of her life. Tommy's wife Shana and their children were the only family Holly had ever known. And she was more grateful for them than she could say.

"Looks like you've got a fan club," Tommy muttered quietly, his deep voice hidden beneath the sweet chords his fingers continued to create.

"What?"

He jerked a nod in the direction of the bar.

A lone man was sitting in the far corner, a bottle of beer in front of him on the table. Even in the dim light Holly could see the stamp of frustration on his features. "Who is he?"

"Can't see from here," Tommy admitted. "Shana says I need new glasses."

Holly chuckled. The room was full of shadows, even with the late-afternoon sunlight spilling through the windows overlooking the street. A gleaming, mahogany bar ran the length of the room, with bottles of every size and shape on the counter behind it, directly in front of a mirror that glittered with reflected sunshine. A second counter ran along the window wall, with plenty of seating for people who wanted to watch the world stroll by as they enjoyed a quiet drink. But mostly, the patrons at the Hotel Marchand bar preferred the small, round, glass-topped tables that crowded the dark wooden floor.

"Doesn't seem like a fan to me," Holly whispered, turning from the man in the corner back to Tommy. "Looks more like Mr. Misery in need of company."

The older man's mouth quirked in a half smile and he winked at her. "You didn't see him when you were singing."

She leaned back against the piano, both forearms braced on its cool, sleek surface. "Liked it, did he?"

"Looked at you like you was the last cool spot on a hot day."

Holly gave him a brief smile. "Flatterer."

"So why'nt you go say hello to the man?"

"Trying to get rid of me?" she teased.

"*Yes*," Tommy said. "Need a little time to myself, girl. Between you and all the women I've got at home…"

She'd heard Tommy's "I'm the only poor male in a household full of women" speech way too many times. To listen to him, a person would never know how much he adored his wife and three daughters.

"I don't know," she said, hiding a smile, "maybe I should just stay here and help you go over the arrangement for the opening song again."

His mouth quirked. "I believe I can manage without your help."

"Possible," she allowed, then narrowed her eyes on the man she thought of as a father. "What I'm wondering is, why all of a sudden you're so willing to see me talking to a man."

Usually, Tommy was more protective than a mother hen fussing over her last chick when it came to any of his "girls."

His long fingers caressed the piano keys, teasing out a soft melody. "I didn't say you should slip off with him. I only said you could go on over and talk to him for a bit. Wouldn't hurt you to meet people."

"People?" she asked, one eyebrow lifting, "or *men* people?"

He frowned and hit a quick riff of bass notes. "Not like I *want* to see you cozying up to a man. But Shana's worried about you."

Holly sighed. So she'd been a little on the celibate

side for the past three years. That wasn't anything to worry about. But telling Shana Hayes not to worry was absolutely pointless.

"I know," Holly said. "She's even been threatening to set me up on a blind date."

He shuddered. "Seems like talking to this fella would be a lot easier. On all of us."

"Seems like," she said. Focusing on the solitary man at the back of the room, Holly inhaled sharply and told herself that walking across the floor would be a lot easier than living through one of Shana's setups.

She stepped off the raised platform that served as a stage and slowly wound her way through the empty tables. Catching the bartender's eye as she went, she asked, "Could I have some sweet tea when you get a minute, Leo?"

"Sure thing," the burly older man called. "Be there in a sec, Holly."

As she approached the man in the shadows, Holly felt the slam of recognition jolt her. He leaned forward in his chair and she noted his pale blue eyes fixed on her. His wavy jet-black hair fell across his forehead in a tumble and his tanned, muscular forearms were braced on the tabletop.

Parker James.

Holly's stomach jittered a little and she half

wished she'd stayed on the stage to bother Tommy. Heck, even thinking about a blind date was a lot better than talking to this particular man. Parker James was New Orleans royalty. His family had been here since...well, forever.

Parker himself spent a lot of time in the local papers, but that wasn't the only reason Holly knew him. She'd sung at Parker's wedding ten years before. It had been one of her first paid gigs, and she'd been way more nervous than the bride.

Of course, she remembered, the bride hadn't been nervous at all....

HOLLY HAD GONE to the reception venue, a restored plantation house on the river, the night before the wedding. She hadn't had to attend the rehearsal at the church, since she'd only be singing at the reception, and she'd wanted to get a good look at the sound system and to leave a copy of her music with the wedding planner.

As late as it was, she'd had the place pretty much to herself. After meeting with the planner, Holly decided to take a stroll outside to get a feel for the place before the big day and, honestly, to enjoy the surroundings in solitude.

Lush and beautiful, the grounds were quiet on that hot summer night. Birds called softly, crickets chirped and river water lapped at the bank. As she walked, she heard muttered whispers and headed toward the sound, curious. Maybe maintenance staff making sure everything was in order for the next day?

She rounded a large planting of magnolia bushes that bordered a flagstone patio where tables and chairs were already set up for the next day. A woman's soft sigh of pleasure, followed by a muffled groan, swept through the air.

Holly stopped dead, but it was way too late.

There in front of her was the bride, Frannie Le-Bourdais, skirt hiked up, panties off, stretched across a table. But the person making Frannie groan wasn't her groom to be—it was her maid of honor.

Stunned into embarrassed silence, Holly only stood there for a moment or two while Justine DuBois caressed Frannie's abdomen then dipped lower. Holly took a step backward, trying to disappear quickly and quietly. But her foot hit the rung of a chair, which scraped against the flagstones.

Frannie's eyes flew open.

She spotted Holly instantly.

In a blink, passion died, replaced by fury. Shoving Justine to one side, Frannie practically leaped off the table, straightened her skirt and stalked over to where Holly stood, still speechless.

It wasn't that Holly was naive. At twenty, she'd been on her own for four years. She'd seen everything there was to see in New Orleans—but still, she was surprised. Parker James seemed to be everything a woman could want in a man. Clearly, though, Frannie didn't want a man. So if she was a lesbian, why the heck was she marrying Parker?

"What the hell are you doing here?" Frannie demanded, then quickly spoke again without waiting for an answer. "Doesn't matter. What matters is this. If you so much as breathe a word of what you've seen here tonight to Parker...I will make your life a living hell. Do you understand me?"

Holly looked into the woman's cold blue eyes and believed. Though it sounded practically medieval, Frannie's threat was all too real. In a city where family lineage carried a lot of weight, Frannie could make it very difficult for Holly to earn a living with her singing. She could have Holly shut out of private parties, fashionable clubs...anything, really.

Shooting a covert look at Justine, Holly saw the other woman glaring at her with such venom in her gaze, she almost shivered.

"I understand," she said to Frannie. It irritated her to have to bend to one woman's icy will, but the fact was, Frannie had a lot more power than Holly

ever would. And if she wanted to make any of her dreams come true, then she had to play the game that was handed her.

Lifting her chin, Holly added, "The threats really aren't necessary, though. It's none of my business what you do or who you do it with."

Frannie eyed her for a long heartbeat or two, then nodded. "Good. See that it stays that way."

AS THE MEMORY FADED away, Holly wondered if Parker had ever discovered his wife's secrets. Maybe he had, since his divorce had been all over the papers lately.

She stopped at his table, looked down at him and smiled. "Hi," she said softly, "want some company?"

ACTUALLY, PARKER HAD slipped into the nearly empty bar to be alone. His day so far had pretty much been a downhill slide and he wasn't looking to chat. Drawn into the shadows by the lovely redhead's smooth, clear voice, he'd lost himself in the dark, forgetting about the mess his life had become.

Now, though, she was standing in front of him, and he couldn't bring himself to ask her to leave him alone. He leaned back in his chair, folded his arms across his chest and looked up at the woman who only moments ago had enthralled him with her singing. She had gentle curves designed to make a grown man weep, and soft gray eyes that made him wonder what they'd look like in candlelight. A few gold freckles dotted her pale skin, and when she smiled, he noticed a slight dimple in her right cheek.

"I like your singing," he said simply.

"Thanks." She pulled out a chair and sat. When the bartender delivered a tall iced tea with a sprig of mint, she gave the older man a smile that lit up the shadowy room. "And thank *you,* Leo."

"Sure thing," he said, sliding a glance at Parker. "I'll be at the bar if you need me."

As the man walked away, Parker let out a slow whistle. "Your knight in shining armor?"

She smiled and shrugged as she reached for her drink. "Leo's a sweetie. He looks out for me."

"Not an unpleasant job."

"A compliment? How nice."

Parker felt the black mood he'd been carrying around slip off his shoulders. Hard to stay pissed when looking at a woman like this. "I'm guessing you get your share."

"Some," she admitted, "but until today, none delivered by Parker James."

His smile faded. "You know who I am?"

Of course she did. But just for a minute or two, he'd been hoping for a brief, anonymous encounter with a beautiful woman. He should have known better. Ever since he'd filed for divorce from Frannie a few months ago, the local papers had been filled with rumors, gossip and outright lies.

She laughed and stirred her tea idly with a clear straw. "Please. Anyone living in New Orleans would know you. You spend a lot of time in the papers."

"Especially lately," he said ruefully.

"But it's not just that," she said, taking a sip of her tea and shooting him another smile that made her gray eyes actually twinkle. "I met you once before. Ten years ago."

He thought about it for a long moment or two, then it came to him. Looking at her as she sat there smiling at him, he wasn't sure how he could ever have forgotten her. Even briefly. But he hadn't noticed her name on the board outside the bar, and she'd done some maturing since they'd last met. "Now I remember."

She nodded. "I sang at your wedding."

He winced. The wedding he never should have gone through with. "Holly Carlyle. The one bright spot that night. You've…changed."

"Have I?" Her fingers held the straw gently and stirred slowly.

A coil of something hot and unexpected rushed through him, and Parker had to make an effort to get a grip. It had been a long time since he'd felt that punch of need. Certainly he'd never felt it for his wife. Frannie had made it more than plain almost from the first that she wasn't interested in sex. And making love to a woman who showed all the enthusiasm of a board having a nail pounded into it was less than appealing.

Though they'd been married now for ten years, they'd been living separate lives for nearly seven of them. He hadn't bothered to get a divorce because it hadn't seemed necessary. After all, it wasn't as though he were anxious to marry anyone else. Frannie had pretty much soured him on the idea of women in general.

But now, looking at the woman sitting opposite him, Parker felt the first stirrings of real attraction. Hell, he'd been in such a long drought, just flirting felt like a cool drink of water on a hot day. He'd been intrigued watching her walk across the room to join him. Her long legs in those tight black jeans had moved slowly, deliberately.

As her fingers stirred her damn tea, he imagined those long red nails scraping against his skin, and it was all he could do not to reach out and grab her hand.

"You're prettier now," he said.

Amusement flickered in her eyes. "Thanks again, I think." Leaning back in her chair, she studied him for a long moment. "So, Parker James, what brings you to the Hotel Marchand bar in the middle of the afternoon?"

"Your voice," he said simply.

"Another compliment." She acknowledged it with a nod.

"I love jazz," Parker told her. "And you really know your stuff."

"I've been singing for my supper for a long time."

"How long have you worked at the Hotel Marchand?"

"Two or three years," she said, sliding her fingers up and down the damp sides of her glass. "I rehearse here every day, work here four nights a week and sit in at clubs around the city the rest of the time."

"Busy woman."

"Idle hands." She countered with a smile, then said, "I noticed there's a new jazz café opening up a few blocks over. Sign reads Parker's Place. That wouldn't be you, would it?"

"It would," he said, and smiled just thinking about his new business venture. It was something he'd wanted to do for years. Run a place that offered his family's dark, rich coffee and the cool, smooth sounds of the jazz New Orleans was famous for.

"Looks interesting," she admitted. "When's it open?"

"In a few days, hopefully. And then," he added almost to himself, "I won't have to deal with…" He stopped abruptly. Hell, he hadn't come in here looking to talk about his problems. He'd come here to forget about them for a while.

"Deal with what?" she asked quietly, her voice a whisper in the darkness.

"Doesn't matter. You don't want to hear about it."

"Parker James, if you knew me a little better, you'd know I wouldn't ask if I wasn't interested."

He studied her eyes for a long minute or two, and then nodded. Taking hold of his still-cold beer bottle, he idly ran his thumb across the microbrewery label. He'd come into the bar to forget about what was bothering him for a while. To take his mind off the continuous machinations of his almost ex-wife and the demands of his family's coffee business. Yet now he found himself wanting to talk about it.

"I had a meeting with Chef Le Soeur," he said, pausing to take a drink of his beer. "There've been some problems lately with my company's coffee deliveries and the chef was threatening to cancel my contract with the hotel."

"That sounds bad."

He gave her a half smile. "Could have been," he admitted, allowing himself to breathe a little deeper. "But I think I've talked him into giving us another chance."

"That's good then," Holly said. "So why the long face?"

He laughed shortly. "You sure you want to hear all of this?"

She gave a little shrug. "Rehearsal's over and I have nowhere to be until tonight."

Why he was glad to hear that, he couldn't have said. "All right, then. You know I'm in the middle of a divorce."

"All of New Orleans knows that."

"Right. Well," he said softly, "in the settlement, I signed over my share of the import division of the family company to Frannie. But with the higher tariffs on importing, the money's not good enough to suit her. She's trying to say I'm sabotaging my own company to keep her from getting the money she was promised."

"Well, that doesn't make sense," Holly said, confused. "If you sabotage your own company, *everyone* loses."

He tipped his beer bottle at her in salute. "You realize that. Unfortunately, Frannie doesn't. Now my coffee deliveries are being screwed up—delayed or just plain disappearing. For all I know, my soon-to-be ex is behind the problem in an attempt to get back at me."

"Seems like that'd be cutting off her nose to spite her own face, but okay." She stirred her tea again, keeping her gaze on his. "So what do you do?"

"Beats the hell out of me," he admitted. "I had a big promotion lined up with the Marchand family—using James Coffees as the new house blend, but the chef's so pissed off now, I'm going to have to work harder to make that happen." He blew out a breath. "With the shipments getting screwed up lately, it'd probably be better all around if I back out of the family business entirely and let someone else run the deals. That way, Frannie can't try to get at the company because of me."

When he stopped speaking, the silence seemed profound. Only then did he notice that Holly's accompanist had stopped playing the piano and slipped out the side door, leaving him and Holly alone, but for Leo the barman.

"So you're just going to give up?"

He frowned at her. "What?"

"You know, surrender? Throw in the towel? Fly a white flag?"

"I know what give up means," he said tightly. "And I don't see where I have much choice."

"There's always a choice," Holly told him with a shake of her head. "And it seems that right now, you're choosing to let your ex-wife win."

"How's that?"

"Well, you've already decided that your promotion won't work."

"I only said I'd have to work harder to swing it—"

"And you seem ready to leave your family's business because of her—"

"If I do, she can't—"

"When I would think it'd be better to stand up and fight back."

"Is that right?" His hand tightened on the beer bottle. "And you've come to these deep and thoughtful conclusions after—what, three *minutes?*"

"I'm a big believer in going with your instincts."

CHAPTER TWO

INSTINCTS.

Granted, her instincts hadn't always been great, but generally speaking, she'd done better listening to them than ignoring them. Those gut feelings were what had kept her so solitary for the last while, nursing a broken heart.

And at the moment, Holly's instincts were telling her to reach out to Parker James. She could hardly believe it herself, since her track record with men had been so abysmal that she'd avoided any kind of relationship for the last few years. But there it was.

Something about the man called to her. Maybe it was the flash in his blue eyes when he talked about the jazz café he'd soon be opening. Maybe it was the way he seemed to need a friendly ear. And maybe it was because of what she knew about the woman he'd married ten years before.

Instantly she wondered if she should tell him

about what she'd seen on that long-ago night. Would the information help him in his divorce battle? Or would the decade-old truth only serve to hurt him?

Staring into his deep blue eyes, where she could still see the shadows of pain, Holly decided to keep quiet. At least for now.

"Instincts, huh?" he asked wryly after a moment or two. "You may be on to something. If I'd listened to my instincts, I never would have gotten married."

"Why did you?" Holly had, over the last ten years, often wondered what kind of marriage he and Frannie had had. She'd wondered if Parker had ever realized that the woman he supposedly loved wasn't very interested in him. For the first couple of years after their wedding, the two had been staples in the society section of the local newspaper. Then they'd sort of faded from public view. "I mean, why did you marry her?"

He frowned. "That's a long story I don't want to think about."

It was as if a shutter had dropped over his eyes, closing her out, ending this quiet little chat that had given her such a brief insight into a man who'd fascinated her for years. Ever since she'd sung at his wedding…ever since she'd seen his wife-to-be betray him the night before taking her vows, she'd felt a sort of…connection to him.

Silly, but true.

"Sorry," she said, and she was. She'd been enjoying talking to him and already she could see him pulling away, emotionally if not physically. He folded his arms across his broad chest in a classic pose of withdrawal.

"Don't be," he said, but he clearly didn't mean it.

Whatever closeness they'd shared was now over. Holly felt it. Felt that previous connection dissolving. Felt the ease between them fade away, and she was sorry about it. There was just something about this man.

"Well, Parker James," she said, picking up her iced tea and scooting her chair back from the table, "it's been nice talking to you."

"Yeah," he said. "Yeah, it was."

"I suppose I'll be seeing you around?" Reluctant to leave, Holly stood beside the table, looking down at him, and wished she could stay. Wished he would ask her to stay.

"I wouldn't be surprised," he said, standing, too.

He was taller than her, but since she was only five foot five, that wasn't difficult. His open-collared blue shirt displayed a vee of tanned chest that made her want to see more, and Holly knew that she could be in big trouble with this man.

He stretched out one hand and she took it. His long fingers curled around hers and sent a jolt of something electric dazzling up her arm. Butterflies took flight in the pit of her stomach and breath was suddenly hard to come by. Pulling her hand free, Holly found a bright smile to give him and hoped to high heaven that it was enough to cover the sudden fluster she was feeling.

"I'd better move along," she said, and turned to leave—while she still could.

ALONE, PARKER WALKED down Royal Street, still trying to figure out what exactly had happened to him. He hadn't talked so much in years. Scraping one hand through his hair, he shook his head and winced as he thought back on everything he'd confided in Holly Carlyle. He'd told a perfect stranger more about his marriage than he'd ever discussed with his family.

What was it about her? Kind eyes? Easy smile?

"Hell if I know," he muttered, walking around a small knot of people staring up at the back of St. Louis Cathedral. He turned right on St. Ann and headed away from the river and Jackson Square. In no hurry to go back to the office, he decided to drop in on the construction crew at his nearly completed café.

But thoughts of Holly kept nibbling at the edges

of his mind as he stepped off the curb and loped across the street. He paid no attention to the smattering of honking horns or the shouts of irate drivers. Instead he hurried his steps as he skirted the crowds wandering down Bourbon Street. He hardly glanced at the stores as he passed. No time to stop and have a beer, and since he lived here, he wasn't interested in any of the proferred tacky souvenirs. He smiled, though, at the clusters of people wandering up and down the narrow street and sidewalks.

There had never really been a "season" for tourists in New Orleans, except for Mardi Gras, which would reach its climax in a few weeks. Generally speaking, there were always tourists wandering through the French Quarter and the Garden District. Craning their necks, snapping pictures…and, most importantly of all to the economy, spending money.

After Hurricane Katrina, the world had wondered if New Orleans would bounce back. If it *could* bounce back. But Parker had never doubted it. The old city seemed indestructible. Of course, heavy winds and rising waters and breaking levees could leave her wounded and just a little shattered.

But the heart and soul of the city would never be destroyed.

And, Parker thought with a jolt, he'd be opening

his own place in time for the height of this year's Mardi Gras season. Most people thought Mardi Gras only referred to the free-for-all on Fat Tuesday, the day before Ash Wednesday. But ask any local and they'd be happy to tell you that Carnival lasted for weeks, with the celebrating heating up in the last two weeks, when the parades and parties kicked in. And this year, Parker would play a part in welcoming visitors, in making them feel like they belonged—if only for a day or two. He smiled to himself as he pulled his cell phone from his pocket and punched in a phone number.

"James Coffees," the receptionist answered smoothly.

"Hi, Marge," Parker said, watching the people stream past him. "Is my father in?"

"No, Parker. He and your mama went for an early lunch."

He smiled to himself at the mental image of his parents. Still holding hands whenever they were together, still crazy about each other, his parents had set a high bar for marriage. He'd hoped to find that sort of happiness once. He'd married Frannie more or less as a business arrangement. But she'd been fun and flirty and he'd hoped that they would grow together and build a solid marriage. Then he'd discovered just how miserable a *bad* marriage could really be.

"You get everything all straightened out with the chef at the Hotel Marchand?"

Marge's voice brought him back from idle speculation. Frowning, he said, "Tell my father I think it's going to work out. I have a little more convincing to do, but," he added, unwilling to accept defeat, "I think I can pull it off."

"He'll be pleased," she said. "You coming back in now?"

"No. Got a few things to do yet. I'll be an hour or so."

"Take your time, Parker. I'll give your daddy the message."

He closed the phone, turned and headed toward the corner of Dauphine and St. Peter. Here the businesses were clustered together, crouched along sidewalks lined with potted flowers. Scrolled ironwork defined balconies on the second stories of the old buildings and brightly colored flowers spilled from boxes and twined along the rails. The blooms scented the cool afternoon air. Jazz drifted from a window and played lightly on a breeze sliding off the river.

Near the corner, a wide front window glittered in the sunlight. Parker's Place was written in scrolling gold letters across the glass, and the front door stood wide open as if in welcome.

The old building had come through Katrina like a queen. She was far enough from the river to have escaped the flooding, and most of the wind had passed her by, for which Parker was grateful. So much of New Orleans had been tested during that storm. So many lives lost and so much of the city's heart broken.

They'd been lucky with the family business, too. Sure, the offices had taken a beating and they'd lost a fortune in inventory that had been stored on the docks. But considering what others had lost, the James family had come through with only a bad bruise or two.

He stepped into the cool interior of his new place and paused, letting his eyes adjust to the dimmer light. The whine of saws and the conversations of the workmen washed over him. He nodded at a couple of guys as he wandered through what would be the jazz café he'd been dreaming of opening for years.

A hand-carved chair rail ran around the circumference of the room and shone with the careful application of several coats of varnish. A century ago, talented hands had found the beauty in the wood, and

Parker took real pleasure in bringing it back to its original glory.

The stage against the far wall was raised only a few inches off the floor. Low enough that the musicians would feel a part of the crowd and high enough to showcase their abilities under the lights strung along the ceiling. Floor-to-ceiling windows fronted the street, and he hoped that passersby would be enthralled by the view and step inside.

Opposite those windows sat a bank of antique, brass espresso machines. In the overhead light, the brass gleamed like a new promise. The main floor was crowded with small round wood tables, and chairs were turned upside down atop them, their legs jutting into the air.

Just another few days until his grand opening. His stomach pitched and fisted into a tight ball of nerves. He'd been dreaming and thinking about this place for as long as he could remember. Now that the time was here, he had to fight the panic. What if it tanked? What if no one was interested in one more jazz house? What if…

"Okay," he muttered thickly, shoving one hand through his hair distractedly. "No point in worrying about all of that just yet."

Besides, it *would* work. He knew it. Felt it. Already,

Parker could see customers crowding around the tables. He could almost hear the sigh of jazz sliding through the air. And without even trying, he heard Holly's silky voice whisper through his mind.

And just like that, his brain was focused on the pretty redhead again. She'd gotten to him, he had to admit, jamming both hands into his jeans' pockets. Somehow or other in the span of one short conversation, that woman had slipped beneath defenses he'd spent years putting into place.

He remembered her smile, the cool gray of her eyes, the grace of her walk and the way she stirred her iced tea with concentration, as if it were the most important task in the world. Everything about her intrigued him, and damn it, he didn't want to be intrigued.

He'd spent an awful lot of time trying to ignore one woman. He was in no position to get mixed up with yet another one.

Didn't matter that Holly was different from Frannie. They were both female, and the one thing he'd learned over the last ten years was that trusting a female was a sure way to get your teeth kicked in.

Still, his insides tightened and something hot and pulsing roared up in his gut as he remembered the deep, throaty sound of Holly's voice caressing the melody of the song. He remembered how that voice had drawn him into the hotel bar. How he'd been mesmerized enough that he hadn't been able to leave even after she'd finished rehearsing.

"Parker?"

The woman had something. Something he hadn't known he was looking for. Something he didn't *want* to want.

"Yo, Parker!"

Startled out of his thoughts, he turned with a frown to face the contractor. A bull of a man with a barrel chest and hands the size of dinner plates, Joe Billet was staring at him, impatience flashing in his eyes.

"Sorry," Parker muttered. "Just thinking."

"Not real happy thoughts, by the look of it," Joe noted.

"Not particularly. What'd you want, Joe?"

"It's the ladies' room," the other man said, already turning toward the back hall. "We got those brass fittings in there like you wanted. Thought you might want to have a look."

"Right." Parker nodded and followed. Much safer to keep his mind on the café than to let it wander down roads that would only lead to trouble. He ignored the mental image of Holly Carlyle smiling at him and followed his contractor.

LATE-AFTERNOON SUNLIGHT slanted through the kitchen windows of the Hayes' house, making the pale green walls shine with warmth. Holly sniffed the steam rising from the huge stainless-steel pot on the stove and gave the shrimp gumbo a stir.

"Oh, my," she said on a blissful sigh. "Shana, you are the best cook in all of New Orleans."

The woman at the sink laughed, tossed a dish towel over her left shoulder and shook her head. "You're easy to please, missy."

"Not at all." Holly turned from the stove, took a seat at the round, pedestal table and looked around this so-familiar room. White-painted cabinets lined the walls and brass-bottomed pots hung from an iron rack over a center island. The granite counters were scrupulously clean and empty of everything but the ingredients for tonight's supper.

Shana Hayes had no patience with clutter.

Holly looked at Tommy's wife. Her smooth, café-au-lait complexion was unlined and her wide brown eyes sparkled with laughter. Her hair was cropped close to her head and thick gold hoop earrings dangled from her ears. Tall and slim, she wore a pale yellow blouse tucked neatly into the waistband of her black skirt. Her sandals clicked merrily on the linoleum as she walked from the sink to the stove and back again.

"As long as you're sitting there," she said with a quick look, "you can shell some peas for me."

"Yes, ma'am," Holly said, and pulled the colander full of plump fresh peas closer to her. "I met Parker James at the hotel today."

"Tommy told me." Shana's tone was noncommittal, and Holly couldn't tell what she was thinking.

"He did?"

Shana nodded. "Said the two of you were looking mighty cozy."

"Oh." Holly swallowed hard. Funny, but she felt like a teenager being interrogated by her mother. Not so strange, she supposed, since Shana was as close to a real mother as Holly had ever known. "Well."

"He wasn't happy about it."

Holly laughed shortly. "*He's* the one who told me to go over and say hello."

"Yes," Shana said quietly. "But he changed his mind right quick once he realized who the man was."

"So he wanted me to say hello, he just didn't want me to enjoy myself."

"He's a man, honey, they don't often make much sense."

"But he really doesn't have anything to worry

about. Honest." Why would it bother Tommy that she'd had a drink with Parker? And if he had been so all-out concerned, why hadn't he said something to *her?*

"Uh-huh."

"There's nothing to worry about," Holly said, filling the strained silence quickly. "We just talked for a while, that's all."

"Is that right?"

Cocking her head to one side, she looked at the older woman. "Aren't you the one who's been telling me to get out? To mingle? To start dating again?"

"Mingle, yes. Date, yes. But, honey, Parker James is the deep end of the pool. You sure you're ready to jump in?"

"I'm not in *anybody's* pool just yet."

"Not how Tommy tells it."

Apparently, Tommy had had plenty to say. Holly took a breath and blew it out in a rush. "You know, he's even more handsome in person than he is in the papers."

"Is he now?" She turned on the faucet and ran a stream of hot water into the sink.

"He seems…lonely, though."

"Uh-huh."

Holly frowned, popped open a pea pod and

scooped the tiny round peas into a blue ceramic bowl. "He says his wife is trying to ruin his business."

"That right?" Shana squirted dishwashing liquid into the water and bubbles erupted.

"He likes my singing."

Shana laughed at that. "Well, why wouldn't he, honey?"

Holly grinned. "You're prejudiced. You love me."

"That I do," Shana said, turning around to lean back against the counter. Folding her arms across her chest, she crossed her feet at the ankles, tipped her head to one side and said, "You seem awful taken with this man."

"I didn't say that," Holly hedged, though heaven knew she had been thinking about him nonstop since leaving the hotel that afternoon. "Besides, I just met him."

Shana shook her head. "Doesn't take long sometimes. One look at my Tommy and I knew down to the bone that he was the one for me."

"This wasn't like that," Holly said firmly. Taken with Parker? What would be the point? No, this was more like flipping through a magazine, spotting a handsome celebrity and imagining yourself as part of his life.

Parker James was just as far removed from her

world as any of those celebrities were. The James family was *royalty* in New Orleans. And Holly Carlyle was just another nobody.

She didn't even know who her parents had been. She was only two when she'd entered the foster system, and when she'd gotten older, she had tried to learn something about her parents and had come up against a brick wall. All she'd learned was that someone had left her sitting on the steps of a police station and then just walked away.

Holly had spent the next fourteen years bouncing around from one foster-care facility to another. Once, she'd even had a foster family. When she was six, for nearly a year, she'd been part of a family. She'd belonged. But then the couple and their *real* children had moved to Florida and Holly had once again been left behind.

After that, she'd learned not to get her hopes up. By seven, she had come to count only on herself. Most of the people in the system meant well, but they had too many kids to worry about. Too many demands and too little time. Holly had run off as soon as she was old enough to risk being on her own.

Wryly, she grabbed another pea pod and broke it open. No, she wasn't anything like the kind of crowd Parker James moved in. But then, he hadn't found happiness, had he? A more lonely, miserable-looking man she'd never run across.

"I didn't say I was interested in him," she finally murmured.

"You didn't have to, honey," Shana said. "It's written clear across your face for anyone to see."

"Great." She ducked her head, pulled another pod out of the colander and concentrated on shucking the peas.

She heard rather than saw Shana cross the kitchen. She pulled out the chair beside Holly and plopped down onto it, then took one of Holly's hands in hers and gave it a pat. "Honey, you know I love you like you were one of my own."

"I know," Holly said, smiling into Shana's worried eyes.

Tommy and his wife and kids were the only real family Holly had ever known. At one of her first professional gigs, she'd been hired to sing at a college graduation party. The piano player had been Tommy Hayes. They'd worked together seamlessly, as if they'd been destined to perform together. That day was the luckiest of her life. Scared and alone at sixteen, she'd tried to pretend that she had everything under control. But Tommy hadn't been fooled. When the gig was over, he'd taken her home for a good meal.

She'd never really left.

She had her own place now, a second-story apartment in the Garden District. But this old house off Fontainebleau Drive would always be *home* to her. Her heart was here. With her family.

Shana's dark eyes met and held Holly's. "I'm just going to ask you to be careful around that man."

"Shana, I'm not—"

"Hush." Her full lips thinned into a stern line and Holly was treated to the same kind of warning glare Shana gave her fifteen-year-old daughter Kendra when she stayed out too late. "You don't want to go getting mixed up with a man in the middle of a divorce, honey. There's no happiness there for you."

Heat rushed through Holly and she was willing to bet she was blushing like a ten-year-old. "Nobody said anything about getting mixed up with him."

"Honey, it's in your eyes. You're smitten with him."

Holly laughed and squeezed Shana's hand. "*Smitten?* God, I didn't think anyone used that word anymore."

"I do." Shana wasn't smiling. "That man's got problems of his own and you don't need to get yourself into the middle of 'em."

"I know. I only said he was handsome."

"Uh-huh. I *know* that's all you said. But it's not all you're thinking." The front door slammed and Shana looked up and shouted, "T.J.? That you?"

Reprieve, Holly thought, grateful for the interruption.

"It's me, Mama." A twenty-year-old female version of her father, Tommie Hayes Junior—T.J.—popped her head around the corner of the kitchen door and grinned. Her shoulder-length hair, woven into dozens of tiny, bead-bedecked braids, swung out in a thick curtain. "Hey, Holly!" Then she asked her mother, "Supper almost ready?"

"Fifteen minutes. Go up and tell your sisters."

"I will. Daddy home?"

"No, but he should be anytime." Standing, Shana laid one hand on Holly's shoulder. "Go get cleaned up," she said to her eldest daughter.

When they were alone again, Shana looked down at Holly. "You mind what I said."

"Yes, ma'am," Holly whispered, then shifted her concentration back to her work. One by one, she went through the pods, scooping peas out, filling the ceramic bowl. And as she worked, her mind drifted back to everything Shana had said.

There was no reason for Shana to worry, Holly realized. Nothing would ever happen between her and Parker James. But once in a while, it was nice to daydream.

Nothing wrong with that, was there?

CHAPTER THREE

BY THE NEXT AFTERNOON, Holly had been giving herself a stern talking-to for nearly twenty-four hours. So far, it hadn't helped.

She stepped off the streetcar at Canal and then headed down Bourbon Street for the long walk to the Hotel Marchand. It probably would have been faster to take a cab, but she enjoyed the St. Charles electric streetcars. They cruised every day through the Garden District and the French Quarter, taking visitors to the city on lovely tours of antebellum mansions and delivering the locals to work in the business districts.

The sun was pleasantly warm on her back. Soon enough, the summer would be here with a heat and humidity unlike anywhere else. But for now, the weather was perfect. And the sounds of her own heels clicking against the pavement kept her company while her brain raced.

Despite knowing better, despite the talking-to Shana had given her the night before—despite *everything*—she just couldn't seem to get him out of her mind.

It wasn't only that he was about the best-looking man she'd ever seen. Handsome men were easy enough to find. No, it was more the painful shadows she'd noted in his eyes that called to her.

"The problem is," she murmured, ducking between two people taking pictures of themselves in front of a voodoo store, "you know too much about him."

Well, she knew why his marriage had failed, anyway. She'd often wondered over the years if she'd done the right thing in keeping quiet. Maybe she should have gone to Parker before the ceremony and told him about what she'd seen. But how in heaven did you tell something like that to a perfect stranger?

"No, no," she said with a firm shake of her head. "It wasn't your business then and it's not your business *now*."

A kid on a skateboard whizzed past her and Holly automatically tightened her grip on the straps of her shoulder bag. During Mardi Gras season, there were more purse snatchers out than usual, hoping to score big on tourists.

But even that stray thought couldn't distract her

for long from thoughts of Parker. A curl of something warm and delicious tightened in the pit of her stomach and she enjoyed the feeling. It had been a long time since *any* man had had such an effect.

Lengthening her stride, she smiled to herself and hurried just a bit. If she was late for rehearsal, Tommy would never let her hear the end of it. And besides, she thought slyly, maybe…just maybe…Parker would turn up again.

By the time she reached the hotel, Holly felt like a kid counting down to Christmas. Silly and she knew it. She'd only seen Parker once at the hotel and she had no reason to believe she'd be running into him again anytime soon, but still…

"Afternoon, Miss Holly."

"Hi, Sam." She nodded to the Hotel Marchand's bell captain, who stood talking to one of the younger bellmen. At six foot four, Sam Malloy had silver hair, pale blue eyes and broad shoulders, and stood like a soldier at attention in his red-and-gold uniform. The doorman was busy helping a woman step out of an elegant black town car, so Sam hurried over to Holly.

"Let me get that for you." He reached out to open the front door for Holly and she gave him another smile as she stepped into the cool, dimly lit interior.

The lobby of the Hotel Marchand was immediately welcoming, despite its air of Old World elegance.

As she headed toward the bar, Holly glanced briefly at the elegant, curved staircase leading to the second floor. Just beyond it, a set of French doors led onto a flower-bedecked courtyard that was also accessible from both the restaurant and the bar.

"You're running a little late, aren't you?"

Holly shot a guilty look at the man standing behind the concierge's desk. Luc Carter was grinning at her. Tall, with sandy-blond hair, pale blue eyes and a warm smile, Luc was the perfect hotel concierge, as charming as he was handsome.

Over the past few months Holly had seen him talk crabby guests into smiling and calm a flustered elderly woman who was sure someone had stolen a diamond pendant from her room. It turned out, of course, that the woman had dropped her prized possession behind the dresser…but Luc had managed to forestall her when she'd come sweeping into the lobby demanding a police presence up to and including the FBI.

"I am late, aren't I?" she said with a wince, pausing briefly at the desk. "I guess Tommy's already here?"

Luc grinned and winked. "Started warming up about twenty minutes ago."

Holly sighed. "He's never going to let me hear the end of it. The man is *always* on time. It's like a religion or something to him."

"Funny," Luc said, straightening a stack of maps of New Orleans as he spoke, "he said the same thing about you and being late."

"Now, who're you going to believe," she asked, smiling. "Me? Or Tommy?"

"I always take the word of a beautiful woman," Luc said gallantly.

"You're smooth, I give you that," Holly answered, laughing. She tapped her fingers on the desk, tipped her head to one side and studied him for a moment. "You okay? You seem a little…down."

"Me?" Luc's grin grew wider, as if he were trying to convince her that he was just fine. "No, I'm good."

"Okay," Holly said, "if you say so."

"Honest." He held up one hand in a three-fingered salute, as if swearing to it.

She nodded, said, "See you later," and headed off to start the afternoon's work.

LUC SOBERED as he watched Holly walk away. He'd have to be more careful. Though he and Holly had become friends over the past few months, he'd begun pulling back. Trying to protect himself. Holly was too intuitive. Too adept at reading people. And he couldn't afford to have her read him.

He and Holly had a lot in common. They'd both overcome unfavorable odds to make something of themselves. Of course, Holly's situation had been worse. At least he'd had his mother's love and support.

What would his life have been like if his father had stayed around instead of leaving when Luc was just a little boy? Maybe Pierre would have come back here to New Orleans and claimed what was rightfully his—a part of his family's fortune.

Luc glanced wistfully around the elegant lobby, but found he could no longer feel the resentment and burning desire for revenge that had gotten him into this mess. After working with the Marchands—his father's sister Anne, and his four cousins—he was finding it hard to believe they were the villains he'd expected them to be. And that made what he had to do so much harder.

"Good afternoon," he said, handing a guest his messages from the cubbyhole of an antique armoire behind him. When the man walked away again, Luc was left to his own thoughts once more.

And he wasn't enjoying them.

It had all seemed so simple a few months ago, when Richard and Daniel Corbin approached him about their scheme to force Anne Marchand to sell the hotel. Luc had leaped at the chance to get back at his father's family for kicking Pierre out when he was eighteen. Though it shamed him some to admit it to himself, he'd believed that Anne Marchand had deliberately cut her brother, Pierre, out of her life, even though his father had told him otherwise—that Anne had in fact supported Pierre. It was their mother, Celeste Robichaux, who had destroyed her son's sense of self, his confidence, practically forcing him into a life of drifting and gambling.

Even as Luc thought it through, a voice in the back of his mind argued that Pierre had made his own choices. He'd disappeared from Luc's life when he could have stayed. He could have *tried* to make a good life for his wife and son.

Damn it, he shouldn't be having these doubts or regret becoming involved with Richard and Dan, two less-than-sterling hoteliers he'd worked for in Thailand. He was supposed to be enjoying the thrill of getting even with his father's family, but the only villain in the family was his grandmother, and she had nothing to do with the hotel.

It had been built with the hard work and dreams of Anne and her late husband, Remy.

But Luc was trapped now. Which put him squarely behind the eight ball. He was trapped. He'd made a bargain with the devil and didn't have a clue how to get out of it—or even if he should try.

If he confessed to his aunt Anne that he'd been behind recent mishaps at the hotel, everything from a damaged generator to botched deliveries—mishaps that threatened to affect bookings and place the hotel in grave financial danger—she'd fire him and maybe even have him arrested. And if he backed out of his deal with Daniel and Richard, he knew they would do even worse.

The telephone on his desk rang and jolted him out of his thoughts. He was grateful for the reprieve, however brief it might turn out to be. Snatching up the receiver, he schooled his voice and said, "Concierge, how may I assist you?"

I SHOULDN'T HAVE come back, Parker told himself. He had plenty of things he should be doing instead.

But that afternoon, as he walked into the bar and took a seat at the table he'd claimed the day before, Parker couldn't think of anywhere he'd rather be. Holly's voice reached out to him, sliding inside him, easing away the rough edges, pushing everything else from his mind.

She swayed on stage, her long, auburn hair swinging in a soft arc behind her head. Her voice caressed each note, heartbreaking in its clarity, its ability to sneak into a man and leave him defenseless. Her eyes shone beneath the single spotlight and she seemed to be staring directly at him.

He felt the connection between them across the empty room and a solid punch of desire crashed into him. His body tightened, his mind went blank. All he could see, all he could hear and feel, was the woman on that stage. Her body moved with the rhythm of the song and her voice called to him.

His heartbeat thundering in his chest, Parker fought to find the control that had long been his mainstay. He wasn't a man to jump into anything without careful thought. Without looking at every option from every possible direction. But now…all he wanted was to stalk across the room, sweep her into his arms and carry her off. He wanted…

The song ended, the last note quavering in the stillness as if it had a life of its own. He watched her as she turned to the pianist and whispered something that Parker had no hope of overhearing. The older man frowned slightly, shot a quick look at Parker, then glanced again at Holly. Whatever he said to her wasn't welcome, because she stiffened slightly. But an instant later she was kissing the man's cheek, then stepping off the stage to walk toward Parker.

He stood as she approached and hoped to hell the light in the room was dim enough that she couldn't see for herself just what kind of effect she had on him.

"You came back," she said unnecessarily.

"Couldn't stay away," he said, though he hadn't planned to admit that.

"I'm glad."

He looked past her to the stage. "I don't think your friend's real happy about it."

Holly sighed, glanced back over her shoulder briefly, then turned to Parker again. "He's...worried."

"About me?"

"No," she said with a laugh. "About *me*. Tommy thinks I should keep my distance from you."

That stung. "And what do you think?"

"I'm standing right here, aren't I?"

"So you are," Parker said, avoiding looking at her friend again. "You were great, by the way."

"Thank you, but singing those songs, it's easy to be great."

Parker shook his head. "No, it's not. Jazz needs heart. And your voice is filled with it."

Her eyes widened and a small smile curved her mouth. "I think that may be the nicest compliment

I've ever been given." She waved a hand at the table beside them. "Would you like to sit? Have a drink?"

"Actually…" Parker chanced a quick look at the man still sitting at the piano. If looks could kill, he figured his body would already be cold by now. "I would. But not here."

She nodded, clearly understanding. "Okay, where'd you have in mind?"

"Willing to take a walk with me?"

Tipping her head to one side, she considered him for a couple of heartbeats. "I guess you look trustworthy enough."

"Thanks—even though you did have to think about it for a minute."

"A girl can't be too careful."

"What happened to the 'follow your instincts' approach to life?"

"That still holds. I'm going on the walk, my instincts are only insisting that I step a little cautiously."

His smile slipped away. "You'll be safe with me," he said, then nodded in the direction of Holly's accompanist. "Trust me, I don't want to do anything that would make your friend over there come after me."

"Good plan," she acknowledged. "You should see what he puts his daughters' potential boyfriends through."

Parker held out one hand toward her, and when she took it, he felt a slow burn start within him. Maybe it was a good thing for both of them that she had such a fierce guardian angel.

Outside the hotel, she pulled him to a stop. "So where are we headed?"

"I want to show you something," he said, and realized that this was what he'd had in mind all along. He wanted to show her his café. Wanted to talk her into singing for him at his place.

Now that the notion was front and center in his brain, he loved the idea. He could already see her on the small stage, hear her voice soaring over the crowd. And he could see more, too. Could see himself, leaning over her, kissing her, tasting her...

"That gleam in your eyes interests me," Holly said, interrupting his fantasy as she hooked her arm through his. "So let's go. Show me something."

They took their time, acting like tourists, mingling with the crowds of pedestrians jamming up the sidewalks. A tour group strolled by, led by a thin, pale man dressed all in black and looking like an extra in an Anne Rice movie. Holly and Parker trailed behind, listening to the well-rehearsed patter about a powerful voodoo queen, Marie Laveau, who'd lived in New Orleans a century ago. Most of the tourists were so busy taking pictures and chatting with each other, they missed the tour guide's story, but Holly was listening.

As the group turned onto a side street, she glanced up at Parker. "Do you think Marie Laveau knew that a hundred years later, people would still be talking about her?"

"They say she could predict the future," Parker mused, "so I wouldn't be surprised."

"It'd be nice, wouldn't it?" she asked, "Being remembered, I mean."

"For being a voodoo priestess?" He frowned. "I don't know that that's the claim to fame most people would go for."

"Oh, I don't know." Holly smiled. "Marie was powerful at a time when most women had no power at all. And, she wasn't only about voodoo, you know. She nursed hundreds through a Yellow Fever epidemic— and lost seven of her own children to the outbreak. She helped the soldiers after the Battle of New Orleans and had a lot of influence over the leaders of the city."

"You seem to know a lot more about her than most people," he teased.

Holly shrugged. "She's fascinating. In fact, I think the whole 'she's evil' thing was started up by men who resented her."

"Possibly."

"The point is, though, she made an impact on this city…on the people. So much so that she's remembered more than a hundred years later. That's pretty impressive."

"True." He steered her around a woman taking a picture of her husband. "And you want to be remembered?"

She laughed. "Doesn't everybody?"

"Never really thought about it."

"I have." She was silent a moment. "But then, with your background I can see why you haven't."

"What's that mean?"

"Easy, big fella," she said, laughing at his defensive tone. "I only meant that the James family's already put their stamp on the city. And you're a part of that."

Parker frowned slightly. He loved his family, but he'd never really been interested in the coffee business. His father lived and breathed the import/export company that Jedediah James had started way back in 1806. He'd done all he could to take James Coffees and build on it—expand it. Parker admired his father for all he'd done, but he just didn't share the same commitment. He didn't want to spend his life working for the family business. He wanted something different. Something that was his and his alone.

He'd worked for his father because it had been expected, but he'd never really put his heart into it. Hell, he'd even gotten *married* because the family expected it. Frannie's family and his had both wanted the match to cement their partnership, something that had never happened.

It shamed him now to remember how lightly he'd entered into the marriage. Frannie was beautiful and charming. She'd made it easy for him to go along with what the families wanted. She'd done everything she could to show him that she was the right woman for him.

At least until they were officially married. Then she'd slowly changed, and Parker had learned just how lonely a man could be.

His marriage had failed and his heart wasn't in his work. The thought of continuing just to be another rung on the James family ladder was a little disquieting.

Frowning, he said, "You're right. Being remembered is important. But more important is what you're remembered for."

CHAPTER FOUR

"IT'S GREAT," Holly said, moving closer to the wide front window. Cupping both hands around her eyes, she leaned into the glass and peeked past the gold letters spelling out Parker's Place.

"You don't have to stare through the window." Parker laughed, took her arm and tugged her toward the front door.

"Good, because I've been dying to get a look at the inside."

Holly stepped across the threshold and paused. Framed prints of old New Orleans dotted the walls. Bare wood floors shone beneath a protective plastic tarp, and overhead, chandeliers made out of antique carriage wheels hung from the ceiling on silver chains that glinted in the late-afternoon sunlight spilling through the window.

Grinning, she weaved her way through the tables toward the stage and stepped onto it to survey the place from an entertainer's perspective. Looking out over the room, imagining throngs of people crowding the small tables, Holly sighed.

"This is going to be wonderful."

"Thanks," Parker said, and she saw the real pleasure on his features. "We're almost ready for opening night."

"Looks like you're ready to roll right now."

Right after she said that, she heard a muttered curse from somewhere in the back, followed by the thunk of something heavy hitting the floor.

Parker winced and shouted, "Everything okay back there, Joe?"

"Fine, fine," a man shouted back, disgust ringing clearly in his tone, "just these blasted copper pipes running from the damn sinks—"

Holly laughed and the sound caressed Parker like a warm summer breeze. Her eyes were shining and the curve of her mouth enticed him. He had to force himself not to go to her. Not to give in to the urge to hold her.

But he wasn't going to get caught by a beautiful woman again. Even one who seemed as guileless as Holly.

"So," she said, "not quite as ready as it looks then, hmm?"

Swallowing back the knot of need clogging his

throat, he joined her on the stage. "Joe's the best contractor in the city. He'll get it all done in time."

"When's the opening?" she asked, scanning the room again.

"Saturday night," he said, trying to see his place through her eyes.

"Planning a big show?"

He shrugged and stuffed both hands into the front pockets of his jeans. "Sort of," he admitted with a half-smile. "I'm not looking for big names to play here. I want it to be more of a neighborhood show-case, you know?"

He glanced at her, caught her nod of understanding and kept talking, enthusiasm coloring his words. "There are so many great jazz musicians in the city, and most of them will never be famous. These are the artists that slip beneath the radar. They play at weddings or birthdays, or on street corners. They deserve a chance to be heard."

"They do," Holly said, her voice soft, dreamy. She stepped off the stage and sat on the edge of it. Crossing her arms atop her knees, she looked up at him. "This is really a great thing you're doing, Parker James."

"Yeah?" He sat beside her.

"Oh, yeah." She sighed and rocked to one side, giving him a friendly nudge with her shoulder.

"When I first started singing, I'd have given anything to play at a place like this."

"When did you start?"

"I can't remember *not* singing, you know?" she mused, tipping her head back to stare up at the stage lights. "But officially, I was sixteen when I first started singing for my supper."

"Sixteen?" He shook his head, trying to remember his own life at sixteen. He'd been the privileged son of a wealthy family, living in a boarding school in England. He'd hated being so far away from home, but every other son in the James family had attended that same boarding school, and tradition was something his family believed in.

He'd never really thought about the advantages his family's wealth had given him. Now that he did, he felt almost guilty.

"At sixteen," he said, "I was playing cricket on a public school field outside London."

She laughed. "London. I'd like to see it sometime myself. When I was sixteen, I got my first long-time gig singing to the late-night drunks at Frenchy's over on Bourbon Street."

"Frenchy's?" Parker gave a low whistle and shook his head slowly. He couldn't imagine someone who looked as delicate and...*fresh* as Holly working

in a dive like Frenchy's. "I know grown men too scared to go into that joint."

"Didn't say I wasn't scared," she pointed out. "But all in all, it wasn't so bad. Frenchy looked out for me. And he let me live above the bar."

"You lived alone? In that neighborhood?"

She shrugged. "I'd have been alone anywhere—and that apartment over Frenchy's was cheap. I had Tommy and Shana, too. I spent a lot of time at their place."

"You're amazing."

"Thanks, but I'm not, really." Holly spoke with a forced lightness. "Trust me. Being out on my own was way better than living in the foster system."

"I'm sorry."

"You don't have to be. It was a long time ago. And I've done just fine."

"How old were you when—"

"I was two." She blew out a breath, rubbed her palms across her knees. "I have no idea who my parents were, but I used to make up some great stories about them."

"Like what?"

"You know, like they died saving me from a fire. Or a crashed plane. Or…"

"You poor kid."

She looked at him warily. "Hey, no point in getting

all sympathetic on me. I'm fine. I like my life just the way it is. Wouldn't change a thing."

"Right. No sympathy." It impressed him that she could dismiss a background that a lot of people would use to garner sympathy. But despite what he'd said, he couldn't help but feel sorry for the abandoned child she'd once been.

Pushing herself to her feet, Holly spun in a slow circle and lifted both hands to encompass the entire room. "Enough about me, Parker. I want to hear more about why you did this. Why it means so much to you."

He stood, too. "Remember what you said earlier? About being remembered?"

"Yeah."

"Well, maybe I don't want to be remembered just for great coffee."

"Makes sense to me."

"Is that right?" he asked, one eyebrow lifting. "Aren't you the one who just yesterday said that I shouldn't quit? Shouldn't just walk away?"

"Well, yeah," she admitted, "but I didn't know that you had this place to turn to. That you had a plan. A *dream*. I mean, I just thought you were, I don't know…just quitting in general."

"That makes a difference?"

"Does to me," she said. "I understand dreams."

"So quitting something as long as you have another goal is okay?"

"Sure, then it's just starting over. That's not walking *away*, it's walking *to*. Makes perfect sense."

He grinned ruefully. "It won't to my parents."

"Not happy about your new venture?"

"They're waiting for me to stop playing at this and concentrate on work again."

"And are you going to?"

"No." He inhaled sharply, deeply, then released the breath on a sigh. "I've been planning this for too long to give it up." He looked from the wide front windows to the espresso machine, to the stage behind them. "This is what I want to do. Run my own place. Maybe sit in on some jazz occasionally."

"You sing?" she asked.

"God, no." He laughed, holding both hands up in surrender. "But I do play the sax a little."

"I'd like to hear you. Nothing like the sound of a good saxophone."

"That could be arranged."

"I like the shine in your eyes when you talk about this place."

"I like the shine in *your* eyes, period," he said, meeting her gaze and holding it as seconds ticked past unnoticed. It was as if everything else in the world drifted away. All he could see, all he *wanted* to see, were her eyes. Like the soft, dreamy gray of fog spilling in off the ocean, they held depths that a man could get lost in.

He knew it was dangerous.

Hell, *stupid,* even.

But Holly Carlyle was the kind of woman a man would find hard to ignore.

Holly held her breath.

There was something here, between them. Had been right from the start. Something electric. Elemental. And if she moved the least bit, she was half-afraid she might shatter whatever spell was holding them in place.

A danger bell started clanging inside her head, but she silenced it.

He lifted one hand to stroke her cheek and Holly felt the heat of his touch sizzle deep within her. She inhaled slowly, hoping the calming breath would steady her. It didn't.

As if from a distance, she could hear the contractor working in the other room. But he might as well have been on Mars. To Holly, it was as if she and Parker were alone on the planet. Her knees went a little wobbly. Her heartbeat quickened in anticipation.

Oh, what she needed at the moment was a freezing-cold shower to douse the flames licking at her insides.

Holly knew better than to give in to the urges that were tearing at her. She'd learned the hard way that she had to be careful when a man made her feel this way. Much more careful than she was being at the moment.

Because right now, all she could think about *was* Parker James's mouth—and wonder if it tasted as good as it looked.

She licked suddenly dry lips. "Are you fixin' to kiss me, Parker James?" she asked, deepening her Southern drawl.

One corner of his mouth tipped up briefly. "I'm thinkin' about it, Holly. How d'you feel about that?"

Well, she was feeling like a fireworks display was going off inside her chest. Nothing she'd experienced before had ever come close to what she was going through right now.

Looking into Parker's eyes, she wanted things she'd never imagined before.

Hot, delicious, *needy* things.

She swallowed hard, slowly reached out and slid both hands up his chest and over his shoulders. She shouldn't. She knew she shouldn't. And she knew just as well she couldn't help herself.

She just had to know if the electricity she'd felt at his touch would intensify when his lips met hers. Deliberately, slowly, she rolled out each word. "I'm feelin' like a little less thinkin' and a little more kissin' might be a good thing."

That mouth of his curved again, and this time she caught a flash of dimples. "My daddy always taught me it was bad manners to argue with a lady."

She moved in closer and nearly sighed as his arms came around her waist. "Your daddy sounds like a very wise man."

"You're still talkin'," he said.

"You best find a way to shut me up, then."

"Do my best."

His mouth came down on hers, and it was as if the world rocked, tilted, then came right again in the space of a single heartbeat.

He must have felt it, too. His arms tightened around her waist, a muffled groan rippled from his throat and he deepened the kiss. His tongue darted past her lips, dipped into her warmth and tasted her passion.

Eyes closed, body electrified, Holly answered his passion with her own. *Never,* she thought wildly, never had she felt anything like this. She hadn't even guessed she *could* feel like this.

His big hands swept up and down her back, his fingers dancing along both sides of her spine. She held on tighter, clinging to him now, meeting his kiss desperately, hungrily. She wanted to feel more. To feel his hands on her skin, his body inside hers. She wanted…too much.

And as soon as that thought splintered her brain, she broke away from him, forcing herself to take a step back. Her mouth was still humming, she could still taste him, smell him, and she locked her knees to keep from bonelessly sinking to the floor.

"Why?" he asked, reaching for her again blindly, his eyes hazy with passion.

"Because," she said, struggling for air, gasping like a landed trout and trying to keep her heart from flying right out of her chest. "Because it's too much. Too fast. And I'm more careful than that."

Nodding, he inhaled and exhaled several times, searching for a calm that was escaping them both. Finally, though, he reached up and dragged his fingers through his hair.

"Okay. Okay, that was fast." The conviction in his voice dared her to deny what he was about to say. "But fast isn't always wrong."

"It is for me," Holly said, though damned if she didn't want to walk right back into his arms. She fit, Holly thought. She fit so neatly against him, as if her body had been sculpted as a perfect match for Parker's. And every part of her was screaming out to feel it again.

But she'd been down this road once before. Okay, fine, it hadn't been this intense, but it was too damn similar to ignore.

"Is that what your instincts are telling you?"

She blew out a breath on a laugh. "Hardly. My instincts are shouting at me to grab hold and enjoy the ride."

"Well, then," he said, one eyebrow lifting.

She shook her head and started talking, wondering, even as she spoke, why she was telling him this. "When it comes to feelings, I'm a little more careful these days. You see, a few years ago, I thought I was in love. He was…like you."

His eyes narrowed. "Meaning?"

"Meaning," she said with a short, harsh laugh, "he was New Orleans royalty. His family was almost as rich as yours and he had about as much in common with me as I do with the Queen of England."

"Oh, for—Holly…"

She held up a hand, closed her eyes briefly and took another breath. "Just—wait. I convinced myself I was in love with him. Got all caught up in the rush of feeling that flash of something hot and reckless…like a summer storm. Lightning-hot and thunder-wild. Turns out, though, while I was thinking about love, he was thinking about killing time."

He took a step toward her, but stopped when she backed up a step. "Damn it—"

"Don't swear at me," she said, a rueful smile twisting her mouth. "I'm telling you exactly how I feel, so you'll know why I do what I do. It's the only fair thing."

"Fine. Be fair. Tell me."

"Not much more to the story," she admitted, though her heart felt a tiny ping of pain, just an echo of what she'd once lived through. "The night I told him I loved him, he caught the first jet out of town. Didn't quit running till he hit Europe. Last I heard, he was still in Paris."

"He was an idiot."

"True," Holly agreed, letting the old hurt slide from her. The signs had all been there. She just hadn't wanted to see them. Jeff had never taken her to meet his family, his friends. They'd always met at her place. Had dinner down in the Quarter, away from everyone he knew. Lessening the odds of stumbling across someone who might recognize him and wonder what he was doing with a jazz-singer nobody.

At the time, she'd told herself he did it because he wanted her all to himself. She'd needed to believe that. She'd wanted so much to belong to someone. To finally matter.

So who was the idiot, really?

"It was just as much my fault as his," she finally said. "Maybe more. I paid no attention to the differences between us. Didn't take into account that my world just never really bumps up against the kind of world he lived in—the kind *you* live in. I mistook heat for caring, lust for love. I won't do that again, Parker. I *can't* do that again."

This time, he came toward her and didn't stop when she eased back. This time, he kept coming, until his hands were on her shoulders, fingers tight. "Nobody said anything about love, Holly. And I'm not asking you to do anything."

"Didn't say you were." Holly lifted her chin to meet him head-on. She had to prove, at least to herself, that she was still strong enough to say no to him, even when looking into those eyes of his. "I'm just letting you know that I won't be swept away again. I won't let heat rush me into a situation I know can't go anywhere."

"So, what you're saying is, you don't trust yourself with me?"

"Oh, please." She scowled at him and only then noted the humor glinting in his eyes. "Fine. Make jokes. But I'm not going to be the easy girl from the wrong side of the tracks for you, Parker James. I won't be another man's secret. His little time-out when his own world gets too stuffy."

"Who the hell said you were?" His hands on her shoulders tightened as he pulled her in close to him. "You've got a lot of ideas in that head of yours, Holly Carlyle, but the ones you've got about me are dead wrong."

"That right?"

"Yeah, that's right." He planted a quick, hard kiss on her mouth, then let her go abruptly. "You've got a problem with my family's money? Then I'd guess that makes you the snob, not me."

She laughed out loud. "Darlin' I don't have enough money to be a snob."

"I'm not the one breaking off a kiss to compare checking accounts."

"I wasn't doing that," she argued, feeling just a little aggrieved now. She was only trying to be honest. To let him know that her attraction to him didn't mean that she would lose herself in a fantasy. Not again.

"Sure you were," he said, shoving both hands into his pockets. "And you ought to know, it doesn't take money to look down your nose at somebody, Holly."

Her mouth dropped open. He couldn't have surprised her more if he'd burst into song and dance. "I wasn't doing anything of the sort."

"Weren't you? Weren't you so busy lumping me in with some jerk who hurt you that you weren't bothering to see me at all?"

"I see you just fine, Parker," she told him. "That's the point."

"No. All you see is the James family. Well, I won't deny I'm a part of that world. But it's not all I am, either."

"I don't know why you're making this so hard."

"I'm not the one who started this," he pointed out.

"I was just trying to tell you how I feel."

"And I'm just saying, why don't you wait a while, see what happens. See if your warning is even necessary."

"No point in waiting if nothing is going to happen," she countered.

"I think something already has and that's why you're running scared."

"I'm not scared, for heaven's sake," she argued, wondering when she'd lost the high ground. Honesty clearly wasn't all it was cracked up to be. She pulled in a deep breath in an attempt to bring her rising temper down a notch or two. "We hardly know each other, Parker. I was only trying to be honest with you."

"Thanks very much," he said. "Consider me warned."

"I didn't mean to start a battle."

"You did a damn fine job accidentally, then."

She shrugged. "It's a gift."

"You're not an easy woman to know, are you?"

"Well, now," she acknowledged, "that's not the first time I've heard that said."

He shook his head, pulled his hands from his pockets and headed to the front door. After he opened it, he paused and looked back at her. "Tell you what. Why don't I walk you back to the Hotel Marchand and you can start figuring out which one of us is doing the most thinking about the 'right' side and the 'wrong' side of the tracks?"

Irritated because there was just the slightest possibility he might have a point, Holly swept past him, then stopped and glanced over her shoulder. "You're a puzzling man, Parker James."

"And you, Holly Carlyle, are a hell of a lot of work."

Despite herself, she smiled. "Maybe, but I'm worth it."

Anger vanished from his eyes, replaced with rueful good humor. "I guess I'll have to find that out for myself, won't I?"

"If you're lucky."

CHAPTER FIVE

"WAIT FOR ME HERE, Jonathon." Frannie LeBourdais James took the hand her driver offered to help her out of the car. Shaking her short, perfectly trimmed blond hair back from her face, she smiled briefly then slipped on a pair of designer sunglasses. "I won't be long."

She wouldn't be here at all, she thought with disgust, if only Parker would cooperate. For pity's sake, she'd been his wife for ten long, very lucrative years. And now he was going through with a divorce? Why? There had to be a reason.

She checked the slim, diamond-studded gold watch on her left wrist, then smoothed one hand down the front of her well-tailored gray slacks. She'd chosen her outfit carefully. Her long-sleeved, dark blue silk shirt hugged her curves and made her blue eyes look like the sea in the morning. She ran her tongue across her lips, moistening the deep pink color she'd so recently applied.

This was an important meeting for her. She'd wanted to look both beautiful and approachable. The one sure way to reach a man—any man, she told herself with an inner smile—was to make him want, to make him need. And then to deny him.

It had been a long time since she and Parker had shared a bed. She frowned, remembering the first couple of years of their marriage, when she'd submitted to his lovemaking and just managed to avoid shuddering.

Not that Parker wasn't a handsome man. He was. She never would have married a troll, no matter the size of his checkbook. But, handsome or not, he simply wasn't what Frannie desired. Not his fault, certainly. But there was no reason she shouldn't remain Mrs. Parker James.

Hadn't her own parents had a very "civilized" arrangement for more than forty years? They both took their pleasure wherever they wanted to—as long as they were discreet. Of course, she thought as she waited for traffic to pass so she could cross the street, she'd made her mistake early on in her marriage. She should have allowed him to make her pregnant. Then she'd have had a chip in the game. He would have stayed with her if she'd only given him a child to carry on the precious James family name.

"Idiot," she muttered, aiming the insult at herself. Such an easy thing and she'd never once considered it.

Why any woman was willing to distort her body and then chain herself to a needy, whimpering child for God knew how long was something she'd never really understood. But if that was what it took to keep Parker married to her...to keep the James family fortune handy...then that's exactly what she would do.

It wasn't too late. She'd just seduce Parker—men really were so easy to handle, after all—get him into bed and let him plant a seed in her. Then she would have a monetary tie to the James family forever. And nowhere was it written that she'd actually have to raise the child herself.

Wasn't that what nannies were for?

Boarding schools?

She smiled at the thought and tapped the tip of one finger against her chin as she imagined how easy it would be to slip herself back into Parker's life.

A break in traffic came just as that last thought skittered through her mind. Frannie grinned. It's a sign, she thought.

She stepped off the curb, glancing at the window that proclaimed Parker's Place, and stopped dead. Shock rippled through her and had her blinking to clear her vision.

But there was nothing wrong with her eyes.

Parker was coming out of his ridiculous little café with a short, curvy redhead. Frannie scrutinized the two of them. Intent on each other, they hadn't noticed her watching.

The woman looked vaguely familiar, but why was that? She leaned into Parker and he smiled at her. That slow, easy smile that Frannie hadn't seen since the first year of their marriage. She could damn near feel the sexual tension pooling around them.

Red-hot anger flared within her, but somehow she kept from storming across the street and tearing the little bitch away from her husband. Instead she stepped back onto the curb and blended into the pedestrians bustling along the sidewalk.

She didn't want to be seen, but she couldn't turn away from the couple. The woman was looking up at Frannie's husband like he was a fresh beignet, and she had to fight the urge to run right over and slap them both senseless. How dare that little bitch go after Parker James? And what in the hell was Parker thinking, smiling and flirting on a public street with a woman who wasn't his wife?

They might be separated, but they were still married. And Frannie wouldn't be humiliated publicly by anyone.

Her breaths came shallow and fast, and a hard knot settled in the pit of her stomach. Her brain raced. Was this the reason Parker was finally demanding a divorce? Had the little redhead somehow latched onto the walking bank account that should be Frannie's?

Just who the hell was she?

How long had this been going on?

And just how involved were they?

Parker and his tramp walked away, and Frannie hissed in a breath. Foolish man. Did he think Frannie LeBourdais would just disappear quietly? Have her life disrupted because all of a sudden he had an itch that needed scratching?

Well, if that was the plan, he didn't know the first thing about her. Still steaming, she turned back to her car. Jonathon reacted instantly, opening the back door and closing it quietly after her. Once he was behind the wheel, Frannie ordered, "Take me to the Café du Monde."

"Yes, ma'am," he said, steering the sleek, black car into traffic.

Ignoring his presence, Frannie flipped her cell phone open, hit number one on the speed dial and waited while the phone rang. At last, a woman answered.

"Justine?" Frannie said. "It's me. You will not believe what I just saw."

Justine rattled off a stream of questions, but Frannie cut her off.

"I'll tell you when I see you. Meet me at du Monde in fifteen minutes, will you?"

Without waiting for an answer, she hung up on her best friend and sometime lover. Then she settled back into the plush leather seat and stared furiously out the window as the city of New Orleans flashed past.

PARKER SPENT the rest of the day at the office.

He wasn't happy about it. He'd rather have been at the jazz café. He'd rather have been with Holly. Hell, he'd rather have been anywhere else but where he was.

Idly, he wondered exactly when the dissatisfaction with his life had begun taking root. He had grown up knowing that one day he would take his place in the family business. He'd worked at the coffee plant as a teenager, starting with a broom and a dust pan. His father believed that the only way a man could understand how a business worked was to do every job at least once.

He hadn't minded working his way up when he was a kid, and getting a corner office at company headquarters was particularly satisfying since he'd known he'd earned it.

Leaning back in the oxblood-leather desk chair, he

swiveled away from the paperwork awaiting his attention, and stared out the window at the harbor. Longshoremen worked steadily on the docks, unloading the latest shipment of coffee beans bound for the James family roasting plant.

And suddenly Parker had the answer to his question. The dissatisfaction had begun when he'd taken over this office. When he'd first studied the view outside this window. It was ten years ago, right before his marriage to Frannie. Parker's father had made him a vice president and presented him with this office.

Parker remembered it all so clearly.

"I'M PROUD OF YOU, boy," his father said, flipping the edges of his suit jacket back to stuff both hands into the pockets of his slacks. "You've done good work here. You've earned this promotion."

"Thanks." Parker wandered around the plush new space. A wet bar sat on one side of the room, and on the other, two leather couches faced each other across a coffee table. A huge desk sat in front of the wide windows that provided a view of the harbor. The gulf stretched out forever and huge ships crawled across its surface. Sunlight glittered on the blue water, reflecting up and into the tinted windows.

"*Your mother wanted to redecorate,*" his father was saying, "*but I thought Frannie would get a charge out of doing it for you.*"

Parker laughed shortly and laid one hand on the cool window glass. "*I don't know if Frannie's interested in decorating, but I'll be sure to ask her.*"

"*Son, I know you're going through with this wedding for the sake of the family, and I want you to know, it's appreciated.*"

"*Uh-huh*"

"*But,*" his father added, then waited until Parker turned to look at him, "*I also know Frannie loves you. Hell, boy, she can't hardly keep her hands off you. And many successful marriages have started with less.*"

"*Don't worry,*" Parker said with a shrug. "*I'm sure Frannie and I will get along fine.*"

"*Sure you will. Your mother and I started out much the same, you know.*" The older man sat on one of the visitor's chairs pulled up in front of the desk. "*Her father and mine negotiated the wedding. Wanted to merge our coffee business and their shipping firm. Worked out fine, I must say.*"

"*I know,*" Parker said, sitting for the first time in the chair where he'd be spending the rest of his life. And while his father continued to reminisce, that

*little phrase repeated itself over and over again in
Parker's mind.* The rest of his life. The rest of his life.

This was it.

This office.

This life.

*He would be a part of the James family coffee
business. He would do what his father had done
before him. He would come to this building, this
office, every weekday from now until eternity. He
would stare out the same window. He would watch
the gulf and the ships coming and going.*

And here he would stay.

Something cold and tight fisted around his heart.

"Your sister's taking over the marketing depart-
ment next year, so I'm thinking the company is in
good hands."

"Seems to be," Parker muttered thickly, reaching
to loosen his tie in an attempt to ease the tightness
in his throat. His breath came short and fast as his
father talked, building plans for the future even while
Parker fought valiantly to survive the present.

PARKER LAID ONE HAND on the window glass. Below
him, on the wharf, it was business as usual. Except
he no longer felt part of it.

He was different now.

He'd put in his time. He'd tried. He'd done his best. Hell, he'd even married the woman his parents had asked him to. Look how well that had turned out.

But now he had something else in his life. The jazz club was something he'd long dreamed about. For his sanity, for his happiness, he would have to turn his back on the dynasty built by his ancestors.

All he had to do now was to break the news to his father.

BY TEN THAT NIGHT, Holly was in the zone.

The crowd at the Hotel Marchand was responsive and she fed off the energy pulsing at her from the shadows. Tommy's talented fingers danced across the piano keys and Tommie Junior was sitting in on bass fiddle. Holly stepped off the stage, taking her cordless mike with her, and walked slowly through the crowd. Easing her way around the tables, she stopped every now and again to lean into a customer and sing solely to him.

She smiled and moved on, then stopped again, listening to the beat, feeling the swell of music fill her, rush through her blood. Every note was like a lover's touch. Every word a promise, and as the spotlight followed her through the room, its heat on her skin felt more natural to her than sunlight.

She caught Leo's eye and he winked at her just before she stopped at a table with a couple celebrating their fiftieth anniversary. The man and his wife leaned in close to each other and smiled up at Holly as she serenaded them briefly before moving on again.

The music continued, one song flowing into the next in a medley that spoke to the heart. This was Holly's favorite part of every evening, mingling with the crowd, smiling and nodding at familiar faces and greeting newcomers.

Wineglasses tinkled and voices murmured just below the swell of the music, and Holly knew she was home. This was where she belonged. The place where she felt most at home. She knew how to work a crowd. She knew how to finesse every chord from a song. She knew how to make every person in the room feel as if they were her guest at a private party.

So many faces turned to her, yet even in the dim light she could distinguish the one she'd least expected to see. Parker James was sitting at what she'd come to think of as "his" table. Alone. At the back of the room.

Watching her.

A jolt of pleasure shot through her, but her voice never faltered. She moved slowly, deliberately, sliding one hand along her waist and over her hip, smoothing the clingy, red-satin dress she wore. Wending her way through the tables, she headed toward him with single-minded determination, the spotlight marking her progress. But all Holly could see was the intensity of Parker's eyes as he watched her.

ALTHOUGH HE HAD SAT in on her rehearsals twice, this was the first time Parker had come to a performance, and it was a completely different experience.

Holly's dress looked as though it had been painted over her curves, the deeply cut neckline emphasizing her breasts, and he could feel his body tightening like a bow string. The music washed over him, but all he could hear was her voice, melodic, hypnotic, reaching deep down inside him to tremble at his core.

When she stopped at his table and smiled down at him, he was lost in the soft light of her eyes, in the sway of her hips, in the sultry sigh of her voice. His heart hammered in his chest and his hands itched to grab her, to pull her onto his lap and hold her there.

As if she could read his mind, she gave him another smile, reached out and trailed the tips of her polished fingernails across his cheek. For one brief, tantalizing moment, time seemed to stop. Something incredible hummed between them, electrifying the air until just drawing a breath spread fire throughout his body.

She felt it, too. He could see that in the flash of surprise in her eyes. Then she turned to make her way back to the stage. He wasn't ashamed to admit that the view as she walked away was just as good as the view of her coming toward him.

She'd gotten inside him, Parker thought. In a couple of days, Holly Carlyle had managed to get under his skin, past the defenses he'd spent the last ten years erecting.

A sobering thought.

One that was troubling enough to douse some of the flames still heating his blood. God knew he wasn't looking for a woman. And yet…he'd needed to be here. To see her again.

To see Holly in her element.

Now that he had, he knew he'd never get her out of his mind again.

Her smile called to him.

Her voice slipped into his soul.

He wanted her.

And more than just the personal—he wanted her singing at his place.

He was businessman enough to realize just what a singer of her caliber, her personality, could bring to his new place. She would bring people in off the streets. Her voice would be a siren song that couldn't be denied.

Somehow, he would have to convince her to sing at his jazz café.

Leaning forward, he braced his arms on the table-top, ordered a beer from the waitress and prepared to wait Holly out. Besides, he couldn't have left now if his life had depended on it.

"YOU DON'T HAVE to take me home," Holly said for what had to be the fifteenth time in the last few minutes.

Parker kept his eyes on the road and his hands fisted on the steering wheel of his black convertible. The sounds and scents of New Orleans assailed them as they drove toward the Garden District.

Disjointed snatches of music drifted from the open doors and windows of the clubs they passed. Neon lights were a blurred rainbow of colors, and in the distance, thunder rumbled over the gulf.

"It's not that far a drive," he said, still not looking at her. Hell, even though she'd changed out of that red dress and into a simple collared shirt and khaki slacks, she was irresistible. Her auburn hair flew about her face and she reached up to gather it and hold it down at the nape of her neck.

"I was surprised to see you at the hotel."

He shrugged. "Wanted to see you at work."

"How'd I do?"

"You were amazing." He shot her a quick look in time to see the pleased smile curve her lips.

"Thank you."

When he stopped for a red light, he finally turned to face her.

"A talent like yours comes along once in a generation. Maybe. Why are you content to stay here and sing in clubs?"

It was hard to tell in the dim light, but Parker was pretty sure she was actually blushing. God, this woman appealed to him on so many levels.

"Well," she said softly, "that's quite a question— and compliment."

"Only the truth."

She smiled at him. "That's kind of you to say. And to answer your question—" she waved her hand to indicate the color and noise of the Quarter "—I love this place. These people. New Orleans is my home. I don't think I'd be happy anywhere else."

"You could still record."

"Don't need to."

"I don't get it. You could be famous."

She shook her head. "I'm not interested in fame."

"Or fortune?"

Holly laughed. "I'm doin' fine, thanks for asking. And I've nearly got enough put away that—"

"That what?"

Her mouth pursed but she shook her head. "Let's just say I've got a few plans and dreams of my own." She pointed. "Light's green."

"Right." Parker stepped on the gas, kept up with the flow of traffic and listened to her as she gave him directions to her place. But even as he listened, one corner of his mind played back what she'd said. What did she dream about? What kinds of plans would grab her, hold on to her?

The streets of the Garden District were sedate after the noise and hubbub of the Quarter. Homes were dark and shadows crouched everywhere.

Moonlight drifted through the trees.

A solitary dog barked and the clang of an iron gate being closed sounded overly loud. The air felt heavy with the scent of night-blooming flowers.

He shut off the engine, got out of the car and walked around to her side to help her out. With her hand in his, he pulled her to her feet and she just sort of naturally ended up pressed against his side. Parker slid one arm around her waist, wanting to hold her there.

"Um, this is my place, here." She stepped back and away, waving one hand at the house on the corner. Two stories, the pale peach building had been standing proud for more than a century. Lacey iron scrollwork defined the upper and lower balconies and gave the old house the look of an elderly woman dressed up in her best.

"Nice," he said, and shoved both hands into his pockets to keep from reaching for her again. "Looks like she came through the hurricane without much trouble."

"It wasn't bad. And I'm on the top floor, so I had fewer problems than most." She started for the black metal gate, worked in the same fashion as the balconies. "I'd invite you in but…"

He nodded. "Probably not a good idea."

"No, probably not."

Leaning back against the hood of his car, Parker said, "I'll be here, till you get inside."

"I'll be fine, Parker. I've been on my own a long time."

"I'll wait, anyway."

She tipped her head to one side and studied him. "How long will you wait? I wonder."

They both knew she was talking about more than his offer to watch until she was safely inside her apartment.

"Guess we'll have to see about that, won't we?"

CHAPTER SIX

HOLLY SAT OUT ON HER balcony for hours after Parker left. The night was cool, but held just a hint of the warmth that would soon cloak the city. She leaned back in her chair, kicked her feet up to the iron railing and crossed them at the ankles.

She took a sip of crisp white wine and stared into the night. A tree hugged the side of the old house, and a slight wind ruffled its leaves, sounding a little like raindrops slapping the street. In the distance, a dog barked halfheartedly, then quieted again.

All around her, the world was sleeping. Holly felt as though she were alone in the universe, and usually she liked that feeling just fine. After all, she was a night owl. She came to life at the same time everyone else was winding down. She liked sitting out here on her tiny balcony, listening to the quiet, feeling the wind, watching shadows stretch across the so familiar street.

It was always peaceful. A relaxing way to end her night and get ready for bed. Until tonight, that is. Tonight her thoughts were too busy ricocheting around her mind for her to relax. And most of those thoughts were—surprise—centered on Parker James.

She couldn't help wondering if she'd made a mistake by not inviting him in. Logically, she knew it had been the right thing to do. The *smart* thing to do. God, she hated being smart. She'd much rather be satisfied. Much rather have him here, now, kissing her in the moonlight. Sighing, she ran her fingers through her hair and tried to ignore the humming in her blood.

"Oh, boy." The sad truth was, Holly wanted Parker as she hadn't wanted anyone since...

"Well, there you go," she whispered into the night. "That's why he's not here right now, missy." She took a sip of wine and shook her head. "If you're going to make mistakes, at least make *new* ones."

The last man who'd turned her inside out, Jeffrey St. Pierre, had come from the same background as Parker. Old money, a lineage that stretched back a century or two and a family that wouldn't be happy about him spending time with a jazz singer.

Jeff had played her for a fool almost from the get-go. And it shamed her to admit just how willing she had been to believe his lies. She had been stupid enough to believe he cared about more than getting her into bed. She'd believed they were headed somewhere—together. She'd told him about her past. Shared with him the plan she had for her future—something she hadn't told anyone else except for Shana and Tommy.

She'd let him into her heart. She'd given him everything he'd needed to shatter her when he'd tired of her. And, oh, that knowledge still stung. Bad enough to have your heart broken. Worse to stand there and invite it.

Another sip of wine and she sighed, as those old memories twisted at her heart one more time. She had learned a lot in the past three years. She'd discovered that she didn't need a man standing beside her to make her happy. She could take care of her own happiness.

She wouldn't allow herself to build dreams that had no hope of coming true.

Not again.

"But, oh, my, Parker surely knows how to kiss," she whispered, fingers tightening on the stem of the crystal glass. She could almost taste him again, his mouth on hers, his breath dusting her cheeks, his heartbeat slamming against hers.

Her stomach did a quick flip and her blood pumped thickly, hotly. The simple truth was, she wanted his hands on her. Wanted his mouth on her.

Wanted him inside her. To feel that rush of sensation that heralded a bone-shaking orgasm.

The question was, would it be smart? No, not really. But as long as her heart wasn't involved, there wouldn't be anything wrong in taking the man to bed, now would there?

Smiling to herself, she drained the rest of her wine, then tapped her toes to the melody stringing out in her mind.

PARKER OPENED his front door the following afternoon and just managed to bite back an impatient oath.

"What's the matter, darling?" Frannie asked as she lifted up on her toes to give his cheek a quick kiss. "Not happy to see me?"

She sailed past him, through the open door, crossed the foyer and stepped into the living room. Dragging the tip of one finger across a long, low table, she idly checked for dust, didn't find any and still smoothed her fingertips together as if rubbing away grime.

"Love what you've done here," she said, though her tone clearly indicated she didn't mean it.

A stab of irritation jolted Parker as he followed his soon-to-be ex-wife into the main room. She wore a pale blue silk dress that clung to her generous curves and stopped about three inches above her knees. He watched her as she did a slow turn, taking in everything.

When he'd moved out of their shared home, he'd done up his new place just the way he wanted it, with oversize, dark brown leather couches and waist-high bookcases all around the circumference of the room. Sunlight glanced in through the wide windows and lay like gold on the pine floorboards.

This was *his* home. Frannie had no place here.

"What do you want?"

"Is that any way to talk to your wife?" She dropped to the edge of one of the sofas and slid one leg over the other.

"*Ex*-wife."

"Not yet, honey." Leaning back into the sofa, she ran the flat of her hand across the soft-as-butter leather. "I don't much care for leather. It can be so uncomfortable in the summer."

He walked into the room and glared at her. "Thankfully, that's not one of your worries."

"Oh, Parker." She gave him a small smile then eased herself off the sofa and walked toward him. "No reason to be hateful, darling. Not when we've shared so much."

Parker laughed. "Who the hell are you playing here, Frannie? The only thing we shared was a name."

She pouted a little and looked up at him from under half-closed eyelids. "Parker, honey, every marriage goes through a little trouble now and then."

Her perfume floated around him, grabbed at his throat, thick, cloying—a lot like Frannie herself. He was immune to her scent. Immune to her lies. But damned if he could figure out what her game was.

"A little trouble?" he repeated. "Frannie, we've been separated for years."

"But still married, darlin'," she purred, holding up her left hand and wiggling her fingers so that the sunlight caught the three-carat diamond and sent sparks of light shooting around the room like balls on a billiard table.

She had always been a fiend for jewelry. The bigger and gaudier, the better.

"I still want to know what you're doing here," he said, stepping away to drag in a breath that wasn't doused in her scent. "We're supposed to meet at the lawyers' office in an hour."

She waved one hand at him and walked to a sideboard that held crystal decanters of vodka, brandy and Irish whiskey. Picking up the vodka, she splashed a small amount into a tumbler and took a quick sip. "I canceled the appointment."

"Why the hell would you do that?"

She smiled. "Parker, honey, we don't need to meet in front of a bunch of lawyers. We can handle this on our own."

"Since when?" He folded his arms across his chest and watched her as she carried her drink back to the sofa and slipped down onto a cushion.

She was up to something. He could damn near see the wheels turning.

"Oh, now, you know as well as I there's not that much to be settled."

True. They had been damn close to signing off on this marriage from hell—until Frannie had decided that her financial settlement wasn't nearly as generous as it should be.

"Only the fact that you want to dip your greedy little hand deeper into my family's company."

Her full lips rounded in a moue that she probably thought of as seductive. Lord knew he'd fallen for that act himself ten years ago. Now he knew better. Now he could recognize the barracuda behind the practiced smile and cooing voice.

"Now, Parker, darlin', I'm sure you'll agree that the settlement we made earlier just isn't fair anymore." She leaned back into the sofa. "Why, the tariffs I'm forced to pay are just monstrous."

"Not my fault new regulations came into place.

You agreed to your share of the company and that's all you're getting from me, Frannie." Parker dropped onto the sofa opposite her. "I'm tapped."

FRANNIE BATTLED BACK a ripple of nervousness. He was too...indifferent. Removed from this conversation. From *her*. Even at their worst, she had been able to bring Parker around with a few smiles and maybe a tear or two. Though she was loathe to admit it, he now seemed immune. But she couldn't allow Parker to slip out of her life, taking his name with her. Her own family line went back several generations, but the LeBourdais family fortune had done considerable shrinking over the last fifty years or so. When Frannie married Parker, her lifestyle had changed dramatically.

And, she acknowledged, she'd become complacent over the last ten years. She'd grown accustomed to the easy wealth, the prestige that his family name had given her. She had been able to live exactly as she wanted. Her affairs were discreet—she made sure no one discovered that she preferred women to men. Her own father would disown her if he knew. Such a God-fearing man, he'd slap the letter L on her shirtfront and toss her into the street without so much as a trust fund to keep her warm.

Her separation from Parker hadn't affected her lifestyle at all. But a *divorce* was going to put a serious crimp in her position in New Orleans society. And that was something she would never accept lightly.

After ten years, Parker was suddenly demanding that divorce. Demanding that they put an end to their marriage legally. Why? What had pushed him over the edge? What had made him decide that his freedom from her was worth fighting for? Was that little redhead behind all this?

Well, if she was, Frannie could fight her. And win.

After all, she'd convinced Parker ten years ago that she loved him. How hard would it be to do it again?

She took a long drink, ran her tongue across her top lip then leaned toward him, making sure he got a good glimpse of the pale pink lace bra she wore beneath her dress. "What would you say if I told you I wasn't interested in getting any more money out of you, darlin'?"

He looked skeptical. "I'd wonder what you were up to."

She smiled despite the sting of the insult, set her crystal tumbler down onto the table in front of her and stood. Walking around the table, she sat beside him and ran the tips of her fingers up and down his arm.

"Parker, honey, the truth is, the closer this divorce comes, the more I've been thinking about...well...*us.*"

"Frannie—"

"Now, let me talk for a minute here, and you just listen, all right?" Her fingertips drifted from his arm to his shoulder and down across his chest. She slid them neatly beneath the collar of his shirt and slowly stroked his bare skin.

Parker shifted uneasily.

Frannie hid a smile. Really. Men were just all too simple to manipulate.

"Honey, I don't think we gave us a real chance, do you?"

HE LAUGHED and grabbed her hand, closing his fingers around it tightly. "A chance? We were married ten years, Frannie. That's chance enough for anybody."

She pouted and Parker absently tried to remember just how often she'd used that same routine to try to wheedle her way around him. Too damn often, he thought, unmoved.

"Now you're just bein' stubborn." She leaned in closer, blew softly against his neck, then touched her mouth to the underside of his jaw.

And he felt nothing.

Absolutely nothing.

"Parker, we could start over. Just the two of us. I could be a good wife."

"Maybe," he said, and jerked his head back so that he could look into her eyes. And there he read the truth. There was no passion. No need. "But not to me."

"You're being unreasonable." She straightened her skirt, then hiked the hem just a bit higher on her thighs.

"Frannie, we didn't even share a bed after the first six months of our marriage."

"We could now."

"And what makes now so different?"

"I've changed."

"Not so I've noticed."

"Well, if you're only going to be insulting."

"I'm not trying to insult you," he said, tired now by this whole pointless discussion. "I'm just saying it's done. Let it go."

"I can't." Temper skittered across her eyes. "I won't."

She reached for him, cupped his cheek in the palm of her hand and brought his face to hers. Slanting her mouth over his, she kissed him, putting everything she had into it.

Simple shock kept Parker in place for longer than

he liked. He couldn't help comparing this kiss to the few he'd shared with Holly. Touching Holly was like grabbing hold of a live wire. Being kissed by Frannie was nothing more than a mild irritation. Finally he broke the kiss and pulled back. "Don't do this, Frannie. Don't embarrass yourself."

Stunned, she stared at him. "*Embarrass* myself?" she repeated, standing and fisting her hands at her hips. "You're the one who should be embarrassed. Your *wife* is sitting right beside you, offering herself to you, reminding you of sacred vows, and all you can do is sit there? Why, you've got all the passion of an ice-cold catfish, Parker James. Or is it that you're too interested in your little redhead to pay any attention at all to your wife?"

His eyes narrowed. When Frannie was angry, the truth usually came spewing out. "What the hell are you talking about?"

"I saw you with her yesterday." She flipped her hair back, then smoothed it with a practiced hand. "Out in front of that little club of yours."

Everything inside him went cold and still. "What were you doing at my place?"

"You're my *husband*," she pointed out. "Why shouldn't I come by to see your newest endeavor?

And I certainly did see her. Shame on you, Parker. You could at least have found someone with style."

"Leave Holly out of this."

"Holly?" She laughed harshly and shook her head. "Silly name."

Jaw clenched, Parker refused to rise to the bait. Whatever she had in mind, he wasn't going to play her games anymore.

Frannie shot him an impatient look. "And that new business of yours? Seriously, Parker. A jazz café? Your daddy must be fit to burst. What are you thinking?"

He stood to face her. "I'm thinking it's none of your business what the hell I do, Frannie. Not anymore."

"That's where you're wrong." She looked up into his eyes. Tapping one long nail against the center of his chest, she said, "I don't want this divorce and I'm going to do all I can to stop it."

"There's nothing you can do."

"Don't you believe it."

He'd had enough. He'd tried to be fair, but the only justice Frannie believed in was the kind that weighed in her favor. God, he couldn't believe he'd stayed married for so long to such a woman. What the hell had he been thinking?

He should have filed for divorce after the first miserable six months of their life together. But at the time, it had seemed easier to stay in the marriage. Laziness on his part, he supposed. And the fact that he hadn't wanted to admit to the world what a mistake he'd made. He wasn't a monk, though, and he damn sure wasn't a saint. So occasionally, when he was offered uncomplicated sex from someone other than his wife, he took advantage of the opportunity. It didn't make him proud to be a cheating husband. But since his wife wasn't interested in being a wife, he didn't feel the guilt he should have under other circumstances.

Hell, their marriage had never stood a chance. And it was only his blindness, his ambivalence that had allowed him to go along with it in the first place.

"Frannie," he said with a bone-deep fatigue that dragged on him, "do us both a favor and go home."

"Now, Parker, honey, don't you be saying anything you might come to regret."

He laughed in spite of everything. "*That's* the woman I know. Threats come a lot easier to you than seduction, Frannie."

Her mouth flattened into a thin, grim line. "What's that supposed to mean?"

"It means, do your worst." He grabbed her elbow and steered her across the room toward the front door. He wanted her out of his house. Out of his life. Hell, out of New Orleans if he could find a way to manage it.

"Stop this," she squawked, tugging ineffectually at his grasp. "Let me go."

He kept walking, forcing her along with him. At the front door, he yanked it open and stepped out onto the porch with her.

She shook free of his grasp, then lifted her chin and glared at him. "Parker James, this isn't finished. Not by a long shot."

"Sure it is." He folded his arms across his chest and looked down into her eyes, clearly reading the frustration glittering hotly there. "I'm not losing any more of my family's business to your greed. And I'm not losing one more minute of my life to you, either. So do what you have to. And so will I."

THE NEXT COUPLE of days passed quickly as Parker worked to get the last details at the café taken care of. He wanted everything to be perfect. It wasn't easy, juggling two jobs. He still had responsibilities at James Coffees, so he couldn't spend as much time at his café as he would have preferred. And that was something he'd have to take care of soon.

He wanted the opening night for Parker's Place to knock the socks off the neighborhood. And he needed his place to be a success. Needed to be able to prove to himself and the rest of his family that this wasn't simply a pipe dream.

So he worked, burying himself in details, both at the café and at the office. And every afternoon, he tore himself away from whatever he was doing and made his way to the Hotel Marchand, drawn by the need to see Holly. To be near her.

After that little chat with Frannie, Parker had come to appreciate Holly's openness even more. Her easy smiles and warm heart were like a soothing drink after a long drought. She filled corners in his soul he hadn't even known were there.

And while that worried him a little, he couldn't seem to stay away from her.

"You're getting to be quite the regular," Holly said as she joined him at his table when rehearsal was over.

"I noticed." He smiled. "Leo had my favorite beer waiting for me when I arrived."

She grinned at him, snatched up the bottle and took a drink. "Leo's not the only one who watches for you to get here."

"Good to know," Parker said. "Leo's not really my type."

"That right? Who is?"

"I think you know the answer to that."

"I might. Still nice to hear."

"Well then, I like tall brunettes who can't sing a note."

Her eyebrows lifted and a smile tugged at the corners of her mouth. "I see."

"Of course, redheads with gray eyes and whiskey-smooth voices have their own kind of appeal."

"I stand relieved."

Leo brought her a glass of iced tea, then walked back to the bar.

"I hear Robert LeSoeur's going to be using your coffee as the hotel brand, after all."

"Yeah." Parker smiled and leaned back in his chair. "Only took a week's worth of convincing, but it's all set. Should be great for business. For James Coffees and the Hotel Marchand."

The chef had driven a hard bargain, but Parker had worked it around until the deal suited both parties. He should have been more pleased at his success, but his heart just wasn't in it. Still, it helped to be leaving the family business with a victory.

"How's your café coming along?"

Now this, he could really enjoy talking about. This was what he cared about. What drove him. "We're ready. I hope. Opening night's tomorrow."

"Exciting."

"And a little nerve-racking. I've got a local band playing for the first couple of hours, so they'll be a good draw."

"Really?" she asked, interested. "Who?"

"Hanson's trio."

"Mmm. Good choice." Holly stirred her tea with her straw. "They're a popular group here in the Quarter."

"I know." Still watching her, he asked her the question he'd been wanting to ask her for a couple of days now. "But for the second set, I was thinking what I needed was a solo. Someone with style and grace and a voice that will keep people in their seats all night."

She tipped her head to one side and her hair fell in an auburn curtain he longed to comb his fingers through. "Got anyone in mind?"

"Matter of fact…"

"Anyone I know?"

"Cute," he said, grinning now. God, it was so easy to talk to her. To be with her. "How about it, Holly? Do a set for me on opening night?"

She took a drink of her tea then tapped her fingernails on the tabletop. "Tommy wouldn't be able to accompany me. He promised his wife they could get away for the weekend after our last set here."

"I can provide a piano player," he said. "He won't be as good as Tommy, but…"

"It'll do."

He reached for her hand and covered it with his own. "Then you'll do it?"

"I'm looking forward to it."

CHAPTER SEVEN

THE GRAND OPENING of Parker's Place was a success—even better than Parker had hoped.

He stood in the back of the club, letting his gaze drift over the crowd. Waitstaff moved through the tables, carrying tall, chocolate-colored ceramic mugs filled with all kinds of coffees. Lattes, mochas, cappuccinos—frothy drinks and ice blends topped with whipped cream, caramel syrup and a long, craggy cinnamon stick for stirring. And for those who preferred a different kind of relaxation, there was wine. A fine selection of some of the best domestic whites and reds.

The scent of chicory-based coffee floated on the still air and mingled with the aroma of freshly baked bread, beignets and panini sandwiches. The room was cast in romantic shadows beyond the stage lights shining down on the Hanson trio, who had already brought the crowd to their feet twice.

Parker made eye contact with a few of the patrons as the trio ended their set to another round of applause. This crowd differed from the ones who frequented the bars in the Quarter. There was a sprinkling of tourists, but most of the people sitting in the candlelit darkness, enjoying well-played jazz, were locals.

And that's just what he had been hoping for. He could make money from tourists, but to be a real success, he'd need the support of the people who lived here. People who were looking for a place to go where they wouldn't have to deal with rowdy drunks. A place where they could listen to good music, share conversation and drink the best coffee his family's firm offered.

Pride filled him.

A pride he had never felt no matter how well he had done his job at James Coffees. This place was *his*. His dreams had brought it to life and he knew, suddenly and clearly, that he couldn't go back to working for his family full-time. Just thinking about the familiar office with its ringing phones and clacking keyboards was enough to fill him with dread. He didn't belong there anymore. Maybe he never had.

This was where he needed to be.

Where he *wanted* to be.

"This is wonderful."

Her voice slipped into him like a warm hand on a cold night and Parker turned to look at Holly's upturned face. Her eyes were dazzled and her full lips curved into a smile of such pleasure, he grinned right back at her.

It was good to share this with someone. To have someone else know how much it meant. To appreciate the rightness of it.

"It's going really well."

"I can see that." She turned to look over the crowd and smiled wider when the applause continued for the musicians who were gathering up their instruments. "Wish I'd been able to get here earlier. I love listening to Hanson's stuff."

"Maybe tomorrow. You don't work at the hotel on Sundays, do you?"

She shook her head, but he could see she was taking in every detail of the room, from the flickering candlelight to the overhead chandeliers, set on dimmer switches.

Through the front windows, he saw people wandering the sidewalks, and almost all of them paused long enough to peer inside. He smiled to himself as one of those curious people turned, pushed open the front door and stepped inside.

"Looks like you just got another customer."

"Been happening like that all night," Parker said. "And it will happen a lot more when you get up on that stage."

"How about a cup of coffee first?"

He smiled. "I think we can handle that. And maybe we could talk about having you sing here regularly." As an added enticement he said, "I pay well."

She smiled. "I'm free Sundays, Mondays and Tuesdays," she said. "And I could use the extra money."

"Expensive shopping habits?"

"You could say that."

Clearly she wasn't going to tell him what exactly she wanted the extra money for, and a part of him pulled back from her. Secrets were never good. Hell, if he'd learned nothing else from those years with Frannie, it was that a woman who kept secrets couldn't be trusted. But maybe he was overreacting. Why should she have to tell him anything? He'd only really known Holly a few days. But somehow, it felt like more.

Felt like a part of him had known her forever.

And he wanted to know everything there was to know. Which terrified him as much as it intrigued him.

"So. Buy a girl a cup of coffee?"

"I think we can manage that."

He steered her toward the espresso bar and crooked a finger at one of the waiters.

OUTSIDE THE JAZZ CAFÉ, Frannie stuck to the shadows.

Infuriated by the look on Parker's face as he smiled down at the redhead, she didn't notice the puddle until it was too late. Cold water—and God knew what else—seeped over the sides of her crocodile mules and she grimaced as the clammy sensation crawled through her.

"Ridiculous," she muttered, slapping one hand on the wall of the building so she could shake her right foot free of the water. "Standing on a sidewalk peeking through windows. I'm reduced to *this?*"

The sting of humiliation was still riding her from her visit to Parker. He had brushed her off, dismissed her attempts at seduction with all but a laugh. But she'd had to see for herself just what Parker was up to with this foolish investment of his. A jazz café of all things. As if New Orleans didn't have enough places to go hear jazz? As if people couldn't buy a cup of coffee anywhere?

Irritated, she slanted another look through the glass at the crowd, hunched over the small tables, their faces lit by candlelight.

And she wanted to slap each and every one of them.

If they hadn't shown up for his "grand opening," Parker might have given up on this stupid idea of his. If no one had come to buy his coffee, drink his wine, listen to his music, he might have realized that maybe he was wrong not only about this place, but about a lot of other things, as well.

Maybe he would have given more thought to her and what she wanted.

But people liked to try something new. The crowds wouldn't stay, though, she consoled herself. They'd move on to something better. But that didn't help her now.

Her old friend Justine was right.

It was time to get some real information on little Miss Redhead.

Time to show Parker James that nobody walked out on Frannie LeBourdais.

HOLLY SMILED at the piano player. Parker had been right. The man wasn't as talented as Tommy, but he was pretty close. Close enough that they worked smoothly together. It wasn't the first time she'd sung with someone other than Tommy and it probably wouldn't be the last.

She moved around the small stage, clutching the microphone in her right hand as she let the music fill her again.

It never ceased to amaze her how she came to life when music played. Beneath the lights, she blossomed like a flower under the sun. She was at home here, where she could look out at smiling faces and know they appreciated her and what she could do.

She'd found her talent at an early age and she thanked God for it every night. She loved losing herself in a song, giving everything she had to the lyrics, to the emotions swamping her with every note.

It was a kind of magic, she thought, the way that lyrics and melody could strike a chord in people's hearts. Her voice climbed soulfully with the mournful notes of the old blues song as her attention focused on the man standing at the back of the room. Parker James.

He watched her, his gaze unflinching, as if he were trying to look deep into her soul.

And what, she wondered, would he think if he could see that deeply into her life?

Her past?

The plan she had for her future? Even as her voice caressed every word of the song, a corner of her mind entertained her dream of things to come. The home she hoped to fill with foster children. The chance for a better life that she wanted to offer kids as lost as she had once been.

But even as those thoughts flew through her mind, she knew the answer to her question. He would see just how different the two of them were. He would see that physical attraction, lust, was all they could ever share.

But what was wrong with that?

HE DROVE HER HOME when the café closed.

Parker told himself that he was only being polite. Thanking her for coming to his place and singing on opening night. But it was more.

And they both knew it.

He could still feel the punch of need that had slammed into him when she'd looked into his eyes across that crowded room. When she'd sung her heart out—it seemed just for him. Heat had arced between them, sizzling the atmosphere until he had half expected to see flames flare up.

Now, his body was tight, his mind a blessed blank, and his heart was pounding in his chest like a teenager hoping to get his best girl into the backseat of his daddy's car.

"I enjoyed myself tonight, Parker."

"You were amazing," he said, turning briefly from the road to watch her profile in the dim light.

"Thanks," she said. "It was fun."

"I, uh…" God, he wasn't in shape to raise the question he'd wanted to ask for the last few hours, but it was either that or give in to the urges clamoring inside. "Look, you said that sometimes you take other gigs during the week."

She blinked at him. "Yeah…"

He turned left, steering the car down a shady street where antique streetlights provided faint light. The windows in the houses lining the narrow street were dark, their occupants asleep.

"I want you to sing for me. Regularly."

"Oh. Parker…"

"Think about it." He parked the car in front of her building, turned off the headlights, shut down the engine and set the brake. Then unsnapping his seat belt, he shifted so that he was facing her. "You work four nights at the Hotel Marchand. Great. Fine. But that leaves three nights open."

"Yes, but—"

"You said you take other gigs where you find them. That you can use the extra money."

"Sure—"

"So work for me."

She unhooked her seat belt and turned to face him. The shadows in the car were so thick, he couldn't read her expression to know what she was thinking.

"Why?"

"What?"

"Simple question, Parker. Why do you want me to work for you?"

"Because you're an incredible talent."

"And…"

"And you'll bring in the crowds. People were coming in off the street all night to listen to you."

"Uh-huh, and…"

He shoved one hand through his hair. In the confines of the car, her scent filled him. Something light, vaguely floral with a hint of spice. He heard her breathing quicken and felt his own speed up to match it. Instinctively he leaned toward her and could have sworn heat rippled off her body in waves.

"What is it you want me to say?"

"The truth. And the truth is, you're not so much interested in me singing for you as you are in getting into my bed."

"Not true."

"As it happens," she went on as if he hadn't spoken, "I'm interested in having you in my bed. So I don't need the soft soap. The compliments. I already want you."

He reached for her, grabbed her shoulders and pulled her in close. Her head tipped back and their eyes met. "It wasn't a sales job," he insisted tightly. "I *do* want you to sing for me. Every night that you can. I want you in my club. I want to hear your voice, watch you move, watch you smile."

"Parker—"

"And all of that's got nothing to do with me wanting to make love to you." Even in the shadowy light, she was beautiful. His hands tightened on her shoulders, his thumbs stroking her skin. Need crouched inside him like a tightly leashed beast snarling to be set loose.

She shivered and her tongue smoothed across her bottom lip, the action tugging at him. "I do want you."

"Good." His grip on her gentled a bit, but he didn't let her go. He wanted his hands on her skin, sliding over every square inch of her. "So? You gonna sing for me or not?"

She smiled. "You gonna kiss me or not?"

"Oh, yeah."

His mouth covered hers, and she sighed into him. Her arms came around his neck, pulling him closer, and his tongue tangled with hers in a fast, erotic dance of need that both of them had ignored for days.

He pulled her onto his lap and groaned as her bottom settled against his erection. Every cell in his body was on fire. He felt the flames and welcomed them. It had been so long.

Need swamped him now, roaring through him, rattling his brain and shattering his soul.

She was everything.

Everything he needed.

Everything he wanted.

And lost in the moment, he refused to think beyond this instant in time.

His hands slid beneath the hem of her silky shirt, his fingertips sliding across her skin. He found her bra, a wisp of a thing, yet a barrier he couldn't let stand between them. Still kissing her, tasting her, exploring her, he swept his hands behind her back to deftly undo the hook.

She sighed when he succeeded, then quickly filled his palms with her breasts, flicking her hard, peaked nipples with his thumbs.

Tearing her mouth free of his, she threw her head back and groaned his name as he kneaded her breasts with a firm, sure touch. A whispered sigh slid from her throat, driving his need even higher.

"I have to get you inside, Parker," she whispered, her voice a raspy breath.

"I don't want to let you go long enough," he admitted, dropping one hand to cup her heated core. He stroked her rhythmically, even through the fabric of her slacks, his touch was electrifying.

"Baby," she whispered, licking her lips, lifting her head until she could look into his eyes again, "if you don't get me into my house right quick, we're probably going to get arrested for having sex in a car."

"Tempting," he said, smiling as he saw the flash of hunger in her eyes.

A grin curved her mouth briefly. "Oh, you're right about that," she said, and shifted her hips, rubbing herself against his hand like a cat looking to be stroked. "But this'll be a lot more fun if we're naked."

Fireworks went off behind his eyes, nearly blinding him. "Good point."

She let go of him long enough to reach behind her back and hook her bra again. Then she leaned in to plant a swift, hard kiss on his mouth. "Let's go then."

She scooted off his lap and Parker muffled another groan as she slipped out from under his touch. He ached for her, and damn, that was hard for him to admit. But she'd sneaked in on him. She'd gotten under his skin without even trying, and now he had to have her.

He couldn't sleep without dreaming about her.

Couldn't work without thinking about her.

She opened the car door, grabbed her purse, then shot him a look over her shoulder. "You comin'?"

"Right behind you."

She practically ran up the narrow stone walk to the front porch, and her key was in the lock before he'd stepped up behind her. The door swung open, and once they were inside, Parker turned the lock and followed her up the steep flight of stairs to the second-floor apartment. Another door here. He could feel his insides jumping, jittering, as he waited for her to get that door open.

At last he was stepping into an apartment that looked like a summer garden. Even through a blurred haze of lust, he could see the home she'd made here. The cool green walls and overstuffed yellow sofas. The place looked…cozy. Female. And it smelled like her.

Floral. Spicy.

Holly.

She threw her purse onto a nearby table, dropped her keys beside it, then turned into him. Hooking her arms around his neck, she pulled his mouth down to hers, then kissed him as if her life depended on it.

All thought and reason fled, leaving only the clamoring need to take her. To take all she offered and to give what he could. If there was a part of him that wished for more, he silenced it quickly.

Parker broke the kiss, lifted her shirt up and over her head, then quickly unhooked her bra again. She shimmied out of it, letting the scrap of lace and elastic drop to the floor.

"Beautiful," he whispered, covering her breasts with his hands again. He felt her pebbled nipples burn into his palms, relishing the skip of her breath as he touched her.

"Wow, that's really good," she said, swallowing hard as she kept a grip on his shoulders to steady herself.

"I'm just getting started."

"Good to know." She looked at him. "You're overdressed."

"Guess I am."

She unbuttoned his shirt, and when she was finished, she pushed it off his shoulders and arms, then scraped the tips of her fingers across his chest. He felt heat streaming through him, filling up every empty nook and cranny inside him.

And even as he realized that, Parker pushed the awareness away. He didn't want to know. Didn't want to think about what that might mean later on.

For now, it was enough to touch her and be touched. To know she wanted him as much as he wanted her.

"I need you," she said. "Right now."

"Oh, yeah."

She grabbed his hand and headed for the darkened

hallway and the room beyond. When she stepped inside, she flicked on a switch and a pale wash of light streamed from under a rose-colored lampshade. All Parker saw was the big brass bed with a mountain of pillows stacked against the headboard.

While he watched, Holly undid the button at the waistband of her slacks and pulled down the zipper. Stepping out of her heeled sandals, she kicked them away, then slipped off her slacks and threw them onto a chair. His mouth went dry. She wore only a tiny triangle of black lace suspended by two wispy threads of elastic.

"You're killing me here," he managed to say.

"Oh, Parker, that's not my intention at all," she said, turning to walk to her dresser on the other side of the room.

Frankly, if she said anything else, Parker missed it as his admiring gaze locked on her behind. Holly was open, easy with her nudity, and that was even more of a turn-on for him. He was glad she wasn't insisting on darkness.

Because he really wanted to look at her.

She pulled the top drawer open, reached inside, then pulled out her treasure, holding it up for him to see. A handful of condoms in brightly colored packages.

"Glad to see one of us was prepared," he said,

grateful. He hadn't carried condoms around in his wallet since he was an eager eighteen-year-old, hoping to get lucky.

She walked back toward him, slowing her steps, swaying her hips, clearly knowing he was watching and enjoying the show. She smiled up at him, tossed her hair back and lifted her chin.

"You're still wearing too many clothes, Parker."

"Won't be in a minute or two."

"Why wait?" she teased.

"What's the hurry?" he countered, and reached for her, cupping her breasts, loving the feel of her silky-smooth skin beneath his fingertips. As much as he longed to lose himself in her, he wanted to savor the glorious sensations coursing through him.

She gave a soft moan. "You're really good at that."

"You ain't seen nothing yet."

"Goodie."

Tossing the condoms onto the bookcase beside the bed, she bent over, grabbed a few of the pillows and pushed them aside. Slowly, she stretched across the mattress to remove a few more. That was all Parker could take.

He leaned over her and cupped her behind, then slid one hand beneath the black lace, finding her damp heat and cupping it. "Forget the damn pillows."

She gasped, straightened and leaned against him, parting her thighs to give him more access. "What pillows?"

CHAPTER EIGHT

"YOU SMELL SO damn good," Parker whispered, pressing her breasts to his chest.

Holly grabbed hold of his shoulders and clung to him like a rock climber finally finding a precarious perch. His mouth moved down her throat to her collarbone. His hands slid up and down her back as he bent over her. Her knees backed up against the edge of the mattress and she fought for balance, knowing she probably wouldn't find it.

Not physical balance.

Not emotional.

Not tonight.

And she didn't care.

For the first time in a long time, she wasn't going to think a situation to death. She was simply going to enjoy what she was feeling. Take this night for what it was and relish it, rather than try to turn it into something else.

Parker felt strong and hard and warm, and it had been too long since she'd been touched.

His hands were rough on her body and she wanted them even rougher. She didn't want to be treated as if she were made of some fragile porcelain. She wanted him fast and hard and eager.

She tugged at the waistband of his slacks and he got the message fast. In a few seconds he was out of his clothes and easing her back until she lay across the mattress.

"This," he said, flicking the thin elastic band of her thong, "is making me crazy."

"Then my work here is done."

"Oh, not even close."

His quick grin shot a jolt of awareness through her, and before she'd quite recovered, he flicked his wrist and had her thong down her legs and tossed aside. Then his hands slid up her body, exploring, touching.

Holly gasped for air and stared blindly up at the ceiling as her heartbeat quickened. When Parker grazed her breasts with his mouth, she gripped the sheets in her hands.

Need spiraled up within her as his tongue teased her nipples and his teeth nibbled.

His breath dusted her skin, his mumbled words

floated in the air, and the rosy glow in the room blurred weirdly. She'd never felt anything like this before.

"I've wanted you since the first moment I saw you," he whispered just loud enough for her to hear.

"Me, too," she said softly, reaching down to stroke one hand through his thick hair, comb it through her fingers. "Oh, me, too, Parker."

He lifted his head and moved to kiss her, taking her mouth even as his hands took her body. She met that kiss with a hunger that seemed to be pulling her into an abyss that shimmered with color and light and sound. Her mind blanked out as their tongues twisted and danced together.

Holly arched into his touch, lifting her hips, pushing against his hand, which cupped her damp heat, and strained for the release she knew she could find only with him.

Her hips rocked with his every touch. She felt the cool kiss of the night air on her skin and inhaled the scent of lemon clinging to her sheets. Every sense felt as if it were on overload.

She'd never experienced anything like this.

His thumb brushed her core and she shuddered, tearing her mouth from his....

"Parker!" Her voice broke on his name, tears

blurred her vision as the first bone-jarring climax jolted through her.

Her hips rocked, her back bowed and she looked up into his eyes, his incredible eyes, and rode the wave of sensation.

"Amazing," he murmured, kissing her briefly, sweetly, as her body trembled.

"Just what I was thinking," she managed to say. She cupped his cheek in her palm and pulled his head down to hers. One kiss. Two. Three. Then she smiled. "I want more."

"Glad to hear it." He reached out behind him, snagged one of the condoms she'd left on the bookcase, tore it open and sheathed himself.

In the next instant he was braced over her, hands at either side of her head.

He entered her slowly, languidly, teasing them both, torturing them both, dragging out the anticipated pleasure until it shimmered in the air around them.

"Take me," she whispered, lifting her legs to hook them around his waist. "Take me, Parker, and let me take you."

He groaned tightly and surrendered to the fury within. She surrounded him with heat, and even more, a feeling of completeness. Such an overwhelming sense of rightness.

And that was enough.

For tonight.

He rocked in and out of her, setting a rhythm she matched stroke for stroke. Lowering his head, he claimed a kiss then watched as passion clouded her soft, gray eyes. Watched as she took a breath, held it, then said his name on a long sigh of wonder.

Her body quivered, trembled, and as she clung to him, he let himself go, riding out the last of the tremors with her.

AN HOUR LATER they were sitting naked in bed, sharing a bottle of good red wine.

"Quite a night," she said.

"Been pretty damn good from my point of view."

Holly grinned. "I think that's a compliment."

"Count on it."

"Well, right back atcha."

He grabbed the wine bottle, topped off her glass then did the same for himself. Setting the empty bottle aside, he clinked his glass to hers, and when they'd both taken a drink, he said, "I want you to know that what we have here is separate from me wanting you to sing at my club."

She gave him a long, thoughtful look, then smiled. "Don't worry, Parker. I believe you."

"Good. Because I admire your talent."

She quirked a grin.

"Your *singing* talent," he qualified with an answering smile. "And I still want you working for me at the café."

Holly studied his face for a long minute, then set her glass down on the bookcase and leaned in toward him. Her subconscious had been wrestling with his offer even while she was otherwise occupied. And now she had her answer. She really wanted to take the job he offered. Every extra dollar she managed to tuck away went into the account that would pay for her dreams. And this steady work from Parker would make reaching that dream a lot easier.

"I appreciate it. And…I accept."

"Just like that?"

"What's the matter?" She smiled at him. "Too easy for you?"

"Not at all, I just thought you'd want some time to think about it—"

"Your offer was a good one. I like your place, Parker. I like *you*." She paused, then leaned back. "Oh, don't get that deer-in-the-headlights look."

"I don't have—"

"Hell, Parker. I can see it clear as anything. You're

worried about me giving you a nice little speech about falling in love with you."

"No." He took a drink. "That's not it. It's…"

"Don't worry about it," she said, and kept her voice light to cover any hint of hurt she might be feeling. She'd known going in that Parker James was out of her league. Of course he'd be worried if a nameless singer started getting all dewy-eyed around him. So she'd keep things on an even keel.

"Holly," he said, reaching out and taking one of her hands in his. "I'm coming out of a marriage that was a nightmare."

Guilt poked at her, and one more time she wondered if she should tell Parker what she knew about Frannie. There was no way to know if that knowledge would help him or hurt him, though.

So she kept silent about the past and tried to protect her future. Her heart was set on making that home she'd wanted so much as a child. She would hire a full-time housekeeper/nanny to be at the house when she was working, and she would lavish all the love she'd ever wanted on the children in her care.

Parker wasn't a part of that future—it was best she remembered that.

"I'm not looking for anything from you, Parker, so you can just put that worry out of your head." She turned her hand under his and linked their fingers. "Whatever else we may find together…work is separate. You need a singer and, like I told you before, I can use the extra money."

He smiled. "Got plans?"

"You could say so."

"Care to tell me about them?"

She thought about it for a minute. But she hadn't even told Tommy and Shana what she wanted to do. She'd trusted only one person with that knowledge and he'd betrayed her. Not that she doubted Tommy and Shana for a minute, but until she had her foster home up and running, she was not going to risk sharing her plan with anyone else. A part of her was afraid of jinxing the whole thing. Silly, she knew, to let superstition rule, but why take chances?

And she could see it all so clearly. An old house with a lot of room. A yard. Trees. A garden. And children. As many foster children as she could take in.

Holly had lived in the system. She knew what it was like to not have a place to call your own. And though there were some very good foster parents, there were all too many who didn't care about the children.

She would be the kind of foster parent she'd wanted when she was still a lonely child, hungering for affection. And between her job at the Hotel Marchand and the extra money she could make working for Parker, her dream would come true a lot faster.

"Not talking, huh?" he said softly, tracing the line of her jaw with his fingers.

She blinked. "Sorry. I was just…"

"Thinking about those plans you're not telling me about?"

"Sort of." She smiled at him to take the sting out of her next words. "An incredible bout of sex doesn't mean we're going to start sharing our lives, Parker. Didn't we just decide that?"

He nodded thoughtfully. "You're an intriguing woman, Holly Carlyle."

"I'm glad you think so, Parker James." She took his wineglass, set it beside hers, then moved to straddle him.

"Another plan?" he asked, hands moving to her hips, thumbs stroking her skin.

"This one's a little more immediate," she said, and flicked her thumbnail across his flat nipple. "And one I have no problem telling you about. Or maybe," she said slyly, "I should just *show* you."

He tightened his grip on her and reached blindly for another condom. "So far," he said tightly, "I like this one a lot."

"Yeah?" She bent her head and nibbled at his

bottom lip with gentle tugs that sent sharp jabs of need shooting through her. "Kind of fond of it myself."

She took the condom from him, tore the foil packet open and leaned back, taking his length into her hands.

"Holly…"

"Let me," she said, and tenderly, carefully, seductively, she sheathed him, smoothing the latex down and over the tip of him. She stroked him, watching his eyes close and his jaw tighten.

Her own body quivered with renewed passion. She could hardly believe how quickly she wanted him again.

Lifting up onto her knees, she settled herself over him, taking him inside her until they were joined as closely as possible. His hands gripped her hips as she moved on him. But this time she set the pace. This time, she was the one steering them both toward completion.

She swept her hands up, lifting her hair, letting it fall to her shoulders again in a soft cloud. She twisted her hips on his, increasing the friction between them, stoking the fires licking at them.

PARKER COULDN'T have taken his gaze off her if it had meant his life. She was every woman. She was beautiful and wild and…breathtaking.

As sensations poured through him, he felt something indefinable notch into place inside him. Something he hadn't expected. Something he didn't want.

Something he wasn't entirely sure what to do with.

Then his body took over, shut his brain down, and he surrendered to the moment. To the incredible feelings coursing through him. He was at the edge of madness, and as he stepped over, he took Holly with him.

"CAN YOU BREATHE?" Parker asked after rolling her onto her back. "I'll move once I can."

Holly laughed, stroking his back as he lay collapsed on top of her. "I must be breathing," she finally said, "so don't move on my account."

"Okay then. Good night."

She smacked his back and laughed again. "Oh, no, you don't."

"Hmm?" He lifted his head and grinned down at her.

"Getting comfy?"

"Can't remember ever being comfier." His fingers twined through the hair at her temple and she sighed at the soft, sweet contact.

She shifted beneath him, twisting her hips against his until they were both breathing hard. This was one connection they could share completely.

"Okay, that's even *more* comfy," he admitted through gritted teeth.

"I hear that."

Holly's mind was happily blank, her body deliciously limp. It had been a while since she'd shared her bed with anyone. Actually, it had been since Jeff. He'd so messed with her head and heart, she hadn't been interested in testing the waters again.

But Parker was different.

Different enough that she was willing to take a chance by getting this close to him. Sure, physically close was a far cry from emotionally close, but she felt herself teetering blindly on the edge of taking that next step.

And she so didn't want to.

She wanted to be a modern woman. A woman who could separate sex and affection. And she knew she'd be in far better shape if she simply treated sex as men did. Casual. Enjoyable. Move on.

But she wasn't wired that way.

For Parker's sake, she'd try to keep her heart out of the mix. She just didn't know if she'd be able to pull it off.

"Okay, moving now," he said, dropping a quick kiss on the column of her throat.

"You sure you want to?"

"Nope." He lifted his head, looked down into her eyes and smiled. As he did, he shifted position and gently pulled his body from hers.

Holly groaned softly, then stretched, arms over her head. She smiled, rolled over to face him and admitted, "I'm cold without my human blanket."

One corner of his mouth quirked as he reached for the edge of the quilt and pulled it over her. "This'll have to do till I get back."

"You leaving?"

"Just going into the bathroom. Then the kitchen. Suddenly, I'm starving. Do you have any food?"

Holly laughed, enjoying herself, enjoying him. "Actually, I do. Stuff for sandwiches, anyway."

"Sounds perfect." He leaned in, kissed her, then rolled off the bed and stood. "Damn it."

"What?" Holly pushed herself up onto her elbows, the quilt sliding down her body.

Voice tight, he asked, "Just how old were those condoms?"

Panic flared, but she managed to keep her voice calm as she asked, "Why?"

He looked over his shoulder at her, and even in the dim light, it was easy to read the disbelief in his dark blue eyes. "Because this one broke."

CHAPTER NINE

INSIDES JUMPING, Parker looked at the naked woman stretched out atop the antique quilt and tried to find the pleasure he'd known only moments ago.

But it was gone.

As if it had never been.

God, he was an idiot. Had she set him up somehow?

"What do you mean, *broke?*" she asked.

"Just what I said." He stalked over to the bathroom, flicked on a light that speared into the room behind him. He tossed the remains of the condom away, then turned and stood in the open doorway. Slapping one hand on the doorjamb, he curled his fingers into the wood and held on tight as a few simple truths rocked him.

Despite what he'd hoped, he had to ask himself if, at the most basic level, Holly was no different from Frannie. Both were out for whatever they could get, and apparently neither cared how they went about getting it.

He looked at Holly and his mouth went dry. Fury? Desire? He couldn't be sure.

She sat naked on the edge of the mattress, tugging at the quilt, trying to jerk it up and over her. "It broke? Oh, God…"

"That about covers it."

Her tangled hair fell into her eyes and, clearly annoyed, she pushed it back. "How could the blasted thing break? I mean, the shelf life of a condom has got to be a long one."

"So they *are* old."

"Sort of."

"How old?"

"They've been in my drawer for almost three years."

"Three years."

"Don't say it like it's a millennium. Besides," she argued, "it's not like I've had a lot of reason to go out and stock up on some new ones." Defensive and obviously feeling the same sort of jittery nerves he was, she jumped off the bed, snatched up the quilt and wrapped it around her. Pushing her hair back from her face again with one trembling hand, she muttered, "My last boyfriend left them here. I just never threw them out and—" She stopped talking and glared at him. "Why am I apologizing to you?"

"Funny," he snapped. "Haven't really heard an apology."

She jabbed one finger in his direction. "And you're not going to."

"Well, that's perfect."

"I didn't hear you complaining a few minutes ago," she reminded him.

True. He hadn't been complaining. Or thinking. He sure as hell was now, though. And the thoughts racing through his mind weren't making him any happier than she looked at the moment.

"That was then," he said tightly. "This is now."

She blew out a breath. "This just cannot be happening."

"Man." Parker shook his head as he stalked across the room and grabbed up his slacks. He couldn't believe this. He should have known better than to get close to somebody again. Damn it. He'd been an idiot and now he was going to have to pay the price. Because of *her*.

No.

He corrected himself immediately. This was his own damn fault. He'd made the mistake of letting his hormones drag him around. And why wasn't she as upset about this as he was?

"You're really something," he said.

"I'm guessing you don't mean that in a complimentary way."

"Bingo."

"I don't see why you're so mad," she snapped, kicking one of his shoes at him. "*I'm* the one who should be freaked out here."

"Actually, I was just thinking that. But you're not, are you?" He zipped his slacks, grabbed his socks and tugged them on, talking while he dressed. "You're right. You should be 'freaked out.' But I'm not seeing that." He stared at her for a long minute. "In fact, you don't even look surprised. Now why would that be, I wonder."

She lifted her chin defiantly. "Oh, I'm surprised by a lot of things right now—not the least of which is just how fast you can morph from tender lover to super jerk."

She took a step, stumbled on the quilt, then bent and grabbed a handful of it away from her feet. "If you're *trying* to make me mad, you're doing a good job."

A damn good actress, he thought. He'd hoped she was different. Believed she was someone he could trust. Someone who could share his passion for music and understand the dreams he was trying to build.

But he should have remembered the lessons Frannie had taught him.

"See, that's the thing, Holly. I shouldn't have to try to make you mad. You should be as furious, as concerned, as I am right now. But you're not." He stepped into his shoes, grabbed his shirt and yanked it on. Leaving it hanging open, he closed the distance between them. He grabbed her shoulders and held on tight. Those smoky-gray eyes of hers locked on his face.

"So I have to think you're not upset because you *knew* that condom was going to break. You wanted it to break. Hell, for all I know, you arranged it."

Her eyes widened. "Are you nuts?"

He gave a short bark of laughter. "Nuts, no. Pissed off? Oh, yeah."

She yanked herself free of his grip, and now those gray eyes of hers were like storm clouds, filled with thunder and lightning, just looking for a place to cut loose.

"You wanted me angry? Well you got it, buster." She staggered back just a bit as she fought for balance. Her hair hung down into her eyes and she tossed her head to clear her vision long enough to glare knives at him. "Why would I want to sabotage a condom? Why would I want to risk my own health?"

"Please." Parker stared at her as if he'd never seen her before. And maybe he hadn't. At least, not the real woman beneath the facade. "No doubt you did your homework and somehow found out I'm healthy. What you were planning was, to get pregnant. To trick me into fathering your child."

"What?"

He smirked. "You should work on your delivery. You don't really have 'shocked outrage' nailed yet."

"You bastard."

He flinched at the whispered oath, but buried his guilt under the layers of anger still cloaking his soul. "Ah, now the fury. A little late, but very effective."

"How can you even say that to me?"

He didn't want to look into her eyes. Didn't want to see the hurt there. Didn't want to feel badly about inflicting that pain. Because if he did, he might start forgetting about why he was so pissed. And God knew, he couldn't afford to let down his guard again.

"You're a piece of work," he said, determined to keep the righteous fires burning within. He checked his pants' pockets, then slanted wild glances over the floor until he spotted the keys that had fallen free. Grabbing them, he straightened and gave her a slow, disgusted look. "But damn, you're really good. You almost had me believing—"

"Are you even aware of how insulting you are?"

Her question came in a deliberately calm tone. But he could see her body nearly vibrating with tightly banked emotions.

"I'm suddenly aware of a lot of things."

"I don't think so," Holly said, taking a step toward him. She had to yank the quilt up and out of her way again.

She looked like a rumpled goddess about to toss lightning bolts at a sinner.

"I don't think so at all," she accused him. "You know, birth control isn't a hundred percent effective even at the best of times."

"Maybe," he said tightly, "but it's the first time I've ever seen a condom explode."

Her full, tempting mouth flattened into a grim slash of disappointment. "And so you've cleverly deduced that I somehow engineered that. Wow. You found me out. You discovered my 'evil plan.'" She rubbed her hands together and would have twirled a moustache if she'd had one. "I've been planning this for years. Ever since the last bastard I trusted turned me inside out, in fact. See, he left those condoms behind and I've been saving them for a night just like tonight."

He jerked his chin up. "This isn't a joke."

"No," she said. "It's too important to be a joke.

And now that you've found me out, I think I should get a little applause for how well my 'plan' turned out. I worked like a dog on those condoms, Parker. Every day I put each of them in the microwave for twenty seconds." She held up a hand when he would have spoken. "Not too long, or they'd melt. Just long enough to mess with their molecular structure. To break down the latex content a little at a time so they'd shatter at just the right moment."

He opened his mouth to argue, but she rushed on again before he could. "No, no. I'm just getting to the good part. I waited and planned and schemed. Not just *any* rich man would do, you know. It had to be *you*, because you're just so bloody perfect."

He winced.

"First I seduced you by going to your place of business every day just to stare at you—" She stopped. "Oh, wait. I didn't do that. *You* did."

Parker frowned at that reminder and started to feel just a little uneasy at the way he'd been acting. "Holly…"

But she wasn't finished.

"Then, when the time was just right, I made sure you chose the weakest of the condoms—couldn't leave that to random chance now, could I? Then, all

I had to do was force you to make love to me. To hold you at gunpoint and take advantage of your virtue. You fell right into my wicked clutches."

"Very entertaining." He glared down at her and swallowed back what might have been a very tiny nugget of regret.

"Makes as much sense as your version," she snapped. "Why, it absolutely amazes me that you're able to walk around upright while balancing a head that big on your shoulders."

He didn't want to feel guilty. Didn't want to rethink his position. It made his world a lot safer—a lot more comfortable if he just kept thinking that she'd tricked him. Then he wouldn't have to risk caring. Now what he had to do was get out of here.

"That's it. I'm done. I'm leaving."

"Damn right you are." She stalked past him, kicking the hem of the quilt out of her way as she stomped across the room to the hallway and the living room beyond. He was right behind her.

"And trust me on this, Parker James, if tonight's little episode *does* result in a pregnancy—God help me—I won't ask anything of you."

"Right."

Holly spun around to face him again. She was shaking with the strength of the anger and disappointment and regret rushing through her. How had the night turned into such a mess?

She'd felt, for a few glorious moments, that they'd connected on a deeper level than the physical. But clearly, that had been just her own little fantasy.

"Whatever you think of me," she said, steadying her voice deliberately, "I want you to know I resent everything you said to me tonight. And one of these days, when you wake up and remember what an ass you were—you're going to wish there was a way to apologize to me."

She yanked the door open. "But just so you know…there isn't."

He didn't speak. For a few seconds, it looked as if he wanted to, but then he thought better of it and stormed out. Holly stood at the open door and listened to his hurried footsteps on the stairs and the slam of the door as he left.

Only then did she close her own door, careful not to slam it herself. She turned the lock and leaned back against the solid wood. A well of grief opened up inside her and she closed her eyes against the sharp, sweet ache of it. How did she do it? she wondered. How did she manage to pick men who only wanted to stomp on her heart?

And why did she keep allowing it to happen?

One hand dropped to her flat belly and a shiver danced down her spine. Opening her eyes, she stared up at the ceiling and really thought about what had happened tonight.

Pregnant?

Surely not.

Her luck couldn't possibly be that bad.

"HE LEFT HER apartment in the Garden District at—" the private detective checked his notes "—three forty-three in the morning and went directly to his own residence. He didn't leave again until this morning when he reported to work at James Coffees."

Frannie leaned back in the Louis XIV chair and eyed the man sitting across from her in a splash of morning sunshine. An older man, Antoine Martin was a retired detective from the New Orleans P.D. He'd opened his own investigation firm four years ago and come highly recommended by both Justine and several other friends. He was discreet, thorough and fast.

Of course, the information he was bringing her didn't make Frannie feel like breaking out in song, but it was information she would need if she wanted to hang on to Parker.

And she did.

"Excellent," Frannie said, smiling at the man who sat watching her through careful blue eyes. "Now, I want you to watch the redhead."

"Ms. Carlyle."

"Whatever." She waved an impeccably manicured hand. "Keep an eye on her. See where she goes. Who she sees. What she does when she's not singing. I want to know everything about her…past, present and future."

"Got it." He stood, tucked his phone into his jacket pocket and headed for the front door. "I'll have a report for you in a few days."

"Perfect," she murmured as she lifted her Meissen tea cup and took a delicate sip.

"YOU WOULD HAVE DONE better to stay clear of that man," Shana said, watching Holly with a guarded eye.

"Oh, you don't have to tell me that," Holly assured her, and picked up a still steaming hush puppy. Popping it into her mouth, she chewed, sighed in bliss and shook her head. "Shana, you are the world's best cook."

"So you say every time you want to change the subject."

"Guilty." Holly dropped into her place at the

Hayes' kitchen table. "Don't suppose you'll let me get away with it just this once?"

"Don't suppose I will." Shana set the plate of hush puppies in the center of the table and took a seat opposite Holly. "You think that I can't tell just by looking at you something's changed?"

Holly looked down at the tabletop. To stall, she grabbed another hush puppy and nibbled at it. She hadn't been lying. Shana's hush puppies were phenomenal. "Sometimes you're too intuitive, you know?"

"A mother's best weapon." She folded her hands on the table and waited.

Holly knew Shana's patience. She'd been at the business end of it many times over the years. The woman could outwait anybody. And with just a knowing look from her, the most stoic person in the world would be spilling their guts sooner or later.

The woman had missed her calling. She should have been a police detective. There wouldn't be an unsolved crime in the county. That patience, those steady, knowing eyes, would coerce confessions out of the most hardened criminal.

"You slept with him, didn't you?"

Holly winced. "Sleep wasn't a big part of last night's festivities, but yeah. I did."

"And now you're thinking it was a mistake."

"God, yes." She leaned back in her chair, popped the rest of the fried dough into her mouth and chewed.

"Wouldn't be the first time a woman's made a mistake with a handsome man."

"True enough."

"However, he's not Jeffrey, you know."

Although it shouldn't have, her acuity startled Holly. "Sometimes you're almost eerie."

Shana laughed, a low, throaty sound that rippled through the kitchen and settled over Holly like a warm blanket. This room held so many good memories. The warmth. The family. The laughter and, yes, even the tears spilled here—memories she desperately needed at the moment.

And Shana was at the heart of it all.

"It's not magic, honey. A mother knows when something's wrong with her child. That's all."

In spite of everything, Holly felt a little better.

"I know he's not Jeff," she said softly. "But, well, we had this huge fight after we— After we had sex, something happened and he started shouting and then I yelled back at him and finally, he just left."

"Uh-huh. So now, you're thinking that he's just another Jeffrey. That he set you up, used you and then tossed you aside?"

"No." Holly scowled thoughtfully. "I considered it last night, I'll admit. But by this morning, I knew it wasn't true."

"That's good. Instincts are usually on target."

"My instincts suck," Holly admitted. "I never saw Jeff for what he was."

"You had blinders on back then, girl. You *wanted* to be in love. Wanted that fairy-tale ending most children dream of."

"And now?"

"Now, you weren't looking for love at all. And yet, it seems you found it."

Holly visibly started. "Who said anything about love?"

"I believe that was me."

"It sure as heck wasn't me!" Holly jumped up from her chair as if she'd been scalded. Her insides jittered and twisted, and she slapped one hand to her belly to settle them down a little so she could think.

Of course, that hand on her belly brought other thoughts to life, so settling down didn't seem to be an option.

Pacing helped. The heels of her boots clacked against the linoleum as she marched to the kitchen sink, did an about-face and marched right back again. Brain racing, heart pounding, she kept walking back and forth, over and over again. Through it all, Shana said nothing. She simply sat there, watching her, waiting for Holly to sort out her thoughts and find answers on her own.

At last Holly stopped and leaned against the counter's edge as if she simply didn't have the strength to support her own body.

"I don't want to love him," she said, her voice flat, emotionless.

"I can understand that."

"Seriously, Shana. He's rich, he's irritating. He jumped down my throat last night over something that so wasn't my fault. He wouldn't listen. He said some really ugly things."

"And were you quiet and kind and standing there mutely like a target?"

"No." She smiled wryly. "I gave back as good as I got, but the things he was saying, Shana—it was irrational. He kept accusing me of trying to trap him—" Her lips twisted. "Like he's some great catch that women all over New Orleans are lining up to get a shot at."

"Were you trying to trap him?"

"Of course not!"

"Then why let words spoken in anger define how you're feeling about the man?"

"Because he was an idiot." Her nails tapped indignantly against the countertop.

"True. But if you're looking for someone who never makes mistakes, you're going to be mighty lonely."

"Maybe lonely is better."

Shana snorted. "You don't believe that at all."

"Be easier if I did."

"Nobody said life was easy."

"I thought he was different," Holly muttered, and folded both arms across her chest, holding her hurt close. She could still see Parker's accusing eyes as he'd looked at her. She could still hear his voice and the ugly words he'd thrown at her.

Everything about it hurt.

More than she wanted to admit.

"You thought he was different, but still, a part of you compared him to the man in your past."

"I guess."

"Maybe he was doing the same thing."

"Don't think he has a man in his past," Holly murmured.

"Smart aleck."

Frowning, Holly met Shana's dark, all-seeing eyes. "Why are you on his side?"

"I'm not." Shana stood, walked over to Holly and gave her a tight hug. "I'm on your side. Like always.

I'm just saying that I think there's more to what you're feeling than simple anger. And a lot of it is because of what Jeffrey did to you. What he made you feel."

"That's over and done with."

"I don't think so." Shana cupped Holly's cheeks in her hands. "Oh, he's gone and you don't love him anymore. But he cut you deep. On a level no man had ever touched before. He made you doubt yourself. Made you treat everyone around you with the suspicion you never showed him."

"Maybe."

"And if you continue to judge all men by the measure of the one who hurt you—then he's not over and done with. And you're still letting him decide how you should feel."

Holly sighed and leaned into Shana's comforting embrace. "I hate when you're right."

CHAPTER TEN

TUESDAY MORNING, Parker still felt like a man on the edge.

He hadn't drawn a single easy breath since Saturday night. Since he and Holly had ended their night with a battle. Just remembering everything that had been said made him wish he could change the way things had gone. Change the way things had ended.

He buried himself in work, putting in a full day at James Coffees and overseeing the jazz café every night, and when he finally did manage to get some sleep, he saw Holly's face in his dreams.

Shuffling a stack of papers, he stared down at the printed lines and saw only black smudges against the white. How the hell could he concentrate on anything when he kept seeing Holly's eyes flashing with anger, widening with shock and hurt?

If he could do it, he'd kick his own ass.

Parker dropped the papers, leaned back in his

chair and gave up the pretense of working. Damn it, he'd reacted all wrong that night with Holly. He knew she hadn't planned to have the damn condom break. He knew, logically, that she wasn't the vicious manipulator that Frannie had been. And yet, he couldn't quite make his heart believe that completely.

He owed Holly an apology, but he didn't trust himself to go see her. Because he still wanted her. Besides, after all he'd said to her, there was no way she'd let him get within ten feet of her, anyway. And who could blame her?

He jumped up from his chair and turned to stare out the window, focusing on the expanse of deep blue water that stretched out to the horizon. Banks of storm clouds hovered in the distance, as if gathering their forces for an assault on the city. Whitecaps smashed against the hulls of the ships heading into the harbor.

A storm rose up inside him, as well. For ten years he'd been married to a woman who'd lied with an ease that came with long practice. He'd learned to be distrustful and it wasn't an easy thing to change.

Hell, he wasn't sure it would be a smart move.

Wasn't he entitled to protect himself? To guard his heart?

"Looks like you've got some dark thoughts today."

Parker turned around abruptly and forced a smile as his father entered his office. A short man with a generous belly and an easy smile, Kemper James strolled across the room, hands in pockets, shirt-sleeves rolled up to his elbows.

"Yeah, I guess so."

"Frannie, isn't it?" His father shook his head gloomily, sank into one of the chairs opposite Parker's desk and sighed. "It was a mistake, Parker. Insisting you marry that woman. I want you to know how much your mother and I now regret ever putting you through it."

Parker sat at his desk, tamping down the emotions raging within. "You didn't know. And it's as much my fault as anyone else's. I could have said no."

"You wouldn't have. I knew you'd do as I asked." Scowling, he added, "In my own defense, though, I was sure that the marriage would turn out all right. For both of you. Worked well for your mother and me."

"I know." Parker smiled.

"It was a mistake. All the way around."

"Doesn't matter anymore."

"Of course it matters, boy. Your mother's worried about you, Parker. She says you're not happy and she doesn't know how to help."

"Tell her she doesn't have to worry about me."

"Tell the stars not to shine, son."

"True." Leaning back in his chair, Parker kicked his legs out and crossed his feet at the ankles. "I'm not saying things haven't been hard. But that's changing. Slowly. And I'm okay. Once the divorce is final, I'll be even better."

"Hope so."

So did Parker. Despite reassuring his father, Parker wasn't convinced himself. Not so very long ago, he'd assumed that divorcing Frannie would bring him instant joy. Now he wondered if he could really be happy without Holly in his life.

Damn it.

"How's the new place coming?"

"Great," Parker said, jolted gratefully out of his thoughts by the shift in subject. He smiled for the first time in days. "You and Mom should come by."

Kemper grinned. "We were there on your opening night."

"I didn't see you." Parker was as pleased as he was surprised.

"Not surprising. You couldn't take your eyes off that singer, Holly Carlyle. We came in in the middle of her act. Didn't want to talk to you then—distract you from what you had to do."

"I'm glad you came. It means a lot to me that you did."

"Your singer? She's good."

"Amazing."

"You don't sound real thrilled."

"It's...complicated." He could at least give Holly her due. As a singer, she had no equal.

"Interesting."

Parker knew what his dad was inferring, but he didn't want to talk about his relationship—whatever the hell that was—with Holly. There were too many things he had to sort out on his own.

"Don't make something out of nothing, Dad."

"Am I?"

Unexpectedly, Parker laughed. "You won't give up, will you, Dad."

"Humor me. Tell me what's going on."

"Not yet." Parker stood, shaking his head. "I've got a few things I have to think about. To work out for myself before I can talk about them with anyone."

His father nodded slowly. "Understandable." Lifting one hand, he pointed at his son. "But once you figure it out, we'll talk again."

"Fair enough."

"Well, then." Kemper put his hands on his knees and stood with a muffled groan. "Guess I'd better get to it. There's a meeting with a new distributor and—"

"Dad, wait." One truth hit Parker like a fist. This

had been coming for a long time, and now, he realized, was the moment to deal with it. "There's something else I do need to talk to you about."

"What?"

He took a breath. "I want to quit."

His father looked stunned. "Excuse me?"

Parker knew it wasn't fair to spring this on his dad with no warning, but the surge of relief he felt made him realize he had waited too long already. He needed to make his own path. To step away from the family business, which had never really interested him. To contribute in his own way to the city he loved.

"It's been coming for a long time, Dad." He waved his hand to encompass his office. "I'm just not suited for this anymore."

"You've done fine so far."

"Thanks, but my heart's never been in the family business."

"This is about Frannie, isn't it?"

"Partly. But it will be the best thing for everyone."

"I don't see how," Kemper responded.

Afternoon sunlight sneaked from behind the clouds, casting the room in golden light. For the first time Parker noticed that his father was getting older. The gray hair that swept back from his high forehead was thinning rapidly, and the wrinkles at the corners of his eyes and the sides of his mouth seemed deeper than before.

Age had slipped up on the old man, and Parker felt a stab of worry about the coming years when his parents would be gone.

Time slipped by so damn fast. You could blink and miss a lifetime. If nothing else, that solidified the rightness of his decision. Life was just too short not to do what was important to you.

Coming around the edge of his desk, he dropped one arm around his father's shoulders. "Dad, Frannie's never going to stop trying to get her fingers into the James' family coffers. You know that."

His father grunted and muttered something unintelligible.

"She'll find a way to keep sucking money out of us. And as long as I'm here, a part of the business, she'll believe she has a shot at it. She won't back down."

"The lawyers can handle her."

"Probably. But it only drags this mess out—and, Dad, I want out." He dropped his arm and stepped back. "I want her and my marriage behind me. I want the past over and the future to begin. This is the one way I know to make sure that happens."

His father watched him for a long minute or two

before saying, "This isn't all about Frannie's greed, though, is it?"

"No, it's not."

His dad nodded. "Doesn't make me happy, but I guess I always knew your sister was more interested in the business than you were."

"That's the solid truth." Parker laughed. "You couldn't blast Miranda out of here with dynamite."

"Girl's driving me nuts every day, coming up with some new plan or other for expansion, diversification…" He shook his head, but there was a gleam of pride in his eyes.

"Miranda loves it," Parker said. "I don't."

"You're sure?"

"I am."

"Can't say I'm really surprised. Disappointed, but not surprised." Then his tone changed as he clapped one hand on Parker's shoulder. "We'll worry about all the paperwork later. Don't you have a jazz café to run?"

HOLLY STOOD AT THE BACK of the room, trying to be invisible while she steadied her breathing. Her long black dress molded itself to her body. Swags of silver beads dripped from her earlobes, dusting the tops of her shoulders, and a teardrop-shaped crystal pendant hung from a silver chain around her neck to lay nestled in her cleavage.

She'd done her best to look fabulous.

She wanted to knock Parker's socks off.

Or, she thought grimly, at the very least, to render him speechless. For his own sake. Because so help her, if he started in on his you-trapped-me routine again tonight, she wouldn't be responsible for her actions.

She inhaled, deeply, trying to ease the knot of tension that had tightened at the memory of their last conversation. God, she had been so furious, so hurt, so blindly eager to kick back, she hadn't been able to think straight.

Maybe staying away from him for a few days had been the best thing to do for both of them. Just as coming here now, tonight, was the only thing she could do.

Shana was right. Judging all men by the actions of one wasn't fair. The pain she'd felt at what Jeff had put her through was gone now, and the anger she felt toward Parker was his alone.

But over the last couple of days she'd begun to wonder if everything he'd said to her had been rooted in pain from his own past. Being married to Frannie couldn't have been easy. And if a man was used to being lied to, wouldn't he learn to expect it from everyone?

"God, I have a headache." She rubbed at the spot between her eyes.

Muted conversation from the audience drifted to her undercover of the soft, slow jazz flowing through the room. Overhead, blue light poured down on the entertainers on stage, setting them apart from the crowd. She sighed a little and leaned back against the cold wall. A chill snaked along her naked spine and swirled through her bloodstream.

But the chill was wiped away as another performer took center stage. Parker stepped forward carrying an alto saxophone with a short, curved horn, his big hands moving gently on the sweep of shiny red and brass. The glossy instrument caught the lights and sent reflected sparks into the audience. His long fingers worked the keys, as if preparing himself to play.

He turned and flashed a quick smile at the musicians behind him, then lifted the sax to his mouth.

As he began to play, a soft, warm spotlight sliced through the cool blue and lay across him, highlighting him for the crowd. Holly's stomach did a very weird pitch and roll. His black hair shone under the light, and as he closed his blue eyes and gave himself over to the music, Holly felt her nerves drain away.

She knew just what to do.

She hummed to herself at first, feeling the melody sink inside her, flooding her body with its soul-soothing rhythm. She swayed gently in the shadows as she became the song, responding in a way that never failed to leave her breathless.

And when she had it—when she felt as though the song were coming from her heart, she began to sing. Her voice was soft at first as she found the pace, settling herself around the cool, throaty sounds of Parker's sax. As her voice lifted, soaring along those notes, heads began to turn toward her.

Smiles welcomed her and a smattering of applause rose as she started a slow, sultry walk toward the stage. But Holly saw none of it. Her gaze was fixed on the stage.

On Parker.

Her heartbeat stuttered a bit, but she concentrated on the music, letting it carry her along when her footsteps might have faltered.

He stared at her as she approached, but his playing never wavered. He didn't lose focus. She felt the power of his eyes on her as she neared, and could have sworn she felt heat shimmering out from him in a warm wave that could have been either welcome or fury.

At the moment she didn't care which it was.

Her voice needed no microphone to swell over the crowd. She stepped in between the tables, dragging her fingertips across glossy surfaces, smiling as she poured her soul into her song. And when she stepped onto the stage and stood alongside Parker, it felt...*right*.

Together, they sailed to the end of that song, and together, slid right into another with hardly a break for breath. The musicians behind them raced to keep up. They were young, probably inexperienced, and Holly smiled inwardly, remembering what Parker had told her about hiring neighborhood talent. He was giving them a chance. A place to shine and show what they had.

Holly leaned into Parker, blending her voice with the sexy strains of the sax, and when the song finally ended and they stood together in the soft overhead lights listening to the applause, they saw only each other.

"I DIDN'T EXPECT to see you here," Parker said, stepping behind the coffee bar to pull out two bottles of cold water. He handed her one of them and took a long drink of his own.

"Don't know why not," Holly said. "You did hire me to sing here three nights a week, didn't you?"

"Well, yeah."

"And Tuesday is one of those nights, isn't it?"

"Yeah. So was last night. And the night before. Didn't see you here then."

Nodding, she took a drink of water and then set the bottle on the bar. "That's true. But it took me a couple of days to get past the urge to kick you the minute I saw you."

He leaned his forearms on the bar. "Guess I can't blame you for that."

"Gee," she said with a very small smile, "thanks so much."

He heaved a sigh. "Look. About that night. I said some things…"

"Oh, you said plenty of things."

"You're not gonna make this easy, are you?"

"Any reason why I should?"

"No," he acknowledged. "I guess not. Look, Holly, I'm not proud of how I acted. I shouldn't have said any of what I did."

Behind Holly, the café was buzzing with conversation and laughter, and the air was filled with the scent of dark, rich coffee and fresh beignets. While the musicians took a break, music drifted in from the street.

She considered his words a minute. "Not exactly an apology," she mused. But it was more than she'd expected. Heck, just talking to him was more than she'd expected. She had figured that she'd come in, sing and then have another fight with Parker about being here.

Maybe life would have been easier if she had simply let whatever lay between them fade away with time. But she'd never been one to go for "easy."

"Holly—" He reached for her, then caught himself, folding his hands into fists. "I can't say I'm sorry for what I thought. But I am sorry I said it."

That stung.

No point in denying it, Holly thought.

The fact that Parker still believed she'd set him up, tore at her. But she wouldn't give him the satisfaction of knowing that. From now on, she'd be as cool as the music they both loved. From now on, she'd remember to protect herself even as she tried to open her heart to possibilities.

"I'm glad you're here, though," he said, and his voice sounded as though those few words had cost him.

"Why, Parker? Why are you happy to see me if you really believe I'm all the things you said I was?"

"Because…I've *missed* seeing you, damn it."

She fought past the ache in her heart to force a small smile. "That's something, I guess."

"I hadn't counted on meeting you, Holly." When one of the baristas came too close, Parker sent him a glare that had the kid scurrying back to the other end of the bar. He turned back to Holly and his eyes were dark and stormy. "I wasn't looking for a woman. I wasn't interested in getting involved again."

"That's the thing Parker—" Anger laced her words. "What makes you so sure that I was looking for *you?*"

He frowned. "I didn't think that."

"Sure you did," she countered, leaning in and lowering her voice. "You said it flat-out. You think I set out to land you like a damn catfish." Her voice went even lower. "That I stockpiled condoms until they were old and useless all in the hope that I would get you to use them."

A flash of something that might have been shame flickered in his eyes.

"Well, you can relax, Mr. James." Holly patted his hand once, twice, then picked up her water bottle. "I'm not looking for anything from you. I'm not interested in your money, your business or your name. All I want is the job you offered me."

"Why?"

"Why what?"

"Why would you want to work for me when you're still so clearly pissed off?"

"That would be *my* business," she said tightly.

Holly knew he was struggling to keep control.

"So is the job offer still on the table?"

"Yes."

"Good." She swallowed hard and cleared her throat before trying to speak again. "Then I'll be here three nights a week. Sunday, Monday and Tuesday. I'll sing for you. I'll bring in the customers and you'll give me a check every Tuesday night for my services. You're my employer. That's all. The beginning and end of our 'relationship.' Agreed?"

"Fine."

"Good." She handed him her water bottle, smoothed both hands down her sides and over her hips, then gave her hair a flip. "Now that we've got that settled, I'll just go and see if the boys are ready to play another set."

"Fine."

His blue eyes looked dangerous and his mouth was a grim slash. Maybe she shouldn't have taken satisfaction in setting him straight about a few things. But she had never claimed to be perfect.

And she still had things to say.

"You were wrong," Holly told him, straightening and shaking her head, making her silver earrings flash. "About me. About everything you said."

Parker braced his legs wide apart and folded both arms over his broad chest. "If it's any consolation, I *wanted* to be wrong."

Anger flared up inside her. Apparently she'd fooled herself into thinking she couldn't be hurt by him anymore.

"You know what, Parker? That's just no consolation at all."

CHAPTER ELEVEN

By Saturday morning, tensions between Parker and Holly were still sky-high.

Parker couldn't say why that bothered him.

Hell, he should have been happy. He had the club he'd long dreamed of. He was in the process of withdrawing from the family business. And according to his attorneys, his divorce to Frannie would be final in a couple of months.

So why the hell wasn't he happy?

He parked his car at the curb, turned off the engine and stared up at Holly's apartment. "She's turned me into a damn stalker," he muttered.

He had tried calling her a couple of times. He had even gone to the Hotel Marchand the night before to talk to her there. But she wouldn't see him and he hadn't been able to smooth-talk his way past Tommy to get close enough to change her mind.

She was bound and determined to keep him at a distance, and that should have made him happy, too.

But it didn't.

And he didn't know what *would*.

All he knew for sure was that his world was off balance. Out of kilter. He missed seeing Holly. Missed touching her. Remembering the one night they'd had together before everything had gone straight down the drain was enough to keep him awake all night.

"Gotta talk to her," he said firmly, glaring now at the upper story of the old house on the corner. "Gotta get whatever's between us out in the open so we can both get over it."

The fact that Holly seemed to have gotten over it didn't sit well with him.

When the front door opened and Holly walked out into a splash of sunshine, Parker's heart stopped. She was beautiful under a spotlight, but in daylight, the sun caught the fire in her hair and made it sizzle. Her pale skin seemed luminous and his hands itched to touch her.

She tipped her head back to smile up at the cloudless sky, but when she glanced down and spotted him, she scowled fiercely.

"Damn it." But then he'd hardly expected her to be happy to see him. A part of his brain reminded him that if she reacted this strongly to his being there, maybe she wasn't as "over" him as she pretended.

Pretty slender thread of hope, but at this point, he'd take it.

Climbing out of his car, he walked around it and stepped up onto the sidewalk right in front of her.

"What do you want, Parker?" She checked her wristwatch, then glanced off down the street.

"Who're you looking for?" Irritation spiked inside him as he wondered who she was waiting to meet.

She shot him a look. "I called for a cab. It's late."

"Cab?" He shoved both hands into his jeans' pockets. "Where you headed?"

Sighing, she stared into his eyes. "That's none of your business."

"It's just a question."

"Fine. I'm looking at a house. Satisfied?"

"You're moving?"

"Possibly," she murmured, checking both ways on the street again in disgust. Still no cab.

"Holly," he said, "I need to talk to you."

She sighed. "Parker, it's a nice day. I don't have to worry about anything until I go to work tonight. I'd like to just relax and enjoy it."

"Good idea. I'll help."

"I can't enjoy it if you're here."

"Ouch." He rubbed one hand against his chest. "Nice shot."

She pushed her hair back impatiently. "I'm not trying to hurt you, Parker, I'm just…"

"Trying to get rid of me."

"Well, yeah."

"I've been trying to talk to you for days."

"I know."

"Too scared to hear me out?" He watched as his words hit her and wasn't disappointed to see a flicker of anger in her eyes.

"You don't scare me."

"Prove it."

"For heaven's sake, what are you? Twelve?"

He grinned. It wasn't much, but at least she was talking to him again. Going with it, he made chicken noises.

A smile twitched at the corners of her mouth. "Fine. What is it you want to say? But make it fast, once my cab shows up, I've got to run."

He glanced up and down the quiet street.

"No sign of your cab. How long ago did you call for one?"

"Twenty minutes," she admitted, reaching into her black leather bag and dragging out her cell phone. "I'll just call for another one."

He grabbed her hand and held on, despite the frigid glare she shot at him. "Don't. Let me drive you wherever you're going."

"Parker…"

"It'll give me a chance to talk and you won't be able to run away."

"Who's running?" she countered.

"You have been. And I'm still not sure why that bothers me. Come on. My car's right here. You really want to wait around for another cab?"

She thought about it for a long minute. The toe of her shoe tapped against the sidewalk. "Fine. You can drive me there. I'll call for a cab to pick me up and bring me home."

"Okay," he said, already ushering her toward the car. Of course, he had no intention of letting her call a cab. But they could talk about that later.

LUC SMILED at a hotel guest as she strolled across the lobby. Morning sunlight glittered off the hardwood floors, snatches of conversation drifted to him from the lobby seating area, and the reception desk was crowded with arriving conventioneers.

Life was good at the Hotel Marchand.

When his desk phone rang, he grabbed it and said, "Concierge, how may I assist you?"

"You can come up with something fast."

Just like that, the light in the room dimmed, shadows reached out for him and panic reared up in his gut. Luc's heart slammed against his chest, then damn near stopped. The smile slipping from his face, he turned his back on the hotel lobby and whispered viciously, "Richard? You shouldn't be calling me here."

He glanced over his shoulder, guilt rising up in him. Richard Corbin hadn't contacted him for nearly a week. Luc had almost managed to convince himself that he and his brother Daniel had decided to back down from their plans to take over the Hotel Marchand.

He should have known better.

"Listen up, Mr. Concierge," Richard was saying, his voice a low growl through the phone. "We're running out of time. Mardi Gras's almost here and we're no closer to edging Anne Marchand out of that hotel."

"I'm working on it," Luc insisted.

Richard's next words made Luc's stomach drop.

"There's no getting out of this. You're in deep, buddy, and don't forget it."

Panic gnawed at the edges of Luc's mind. He couldn't see a way out. He didn't have a clue what to do next.

"You'd better come up with some good ideas to

make that bitch sell. Otherwise we'll have to step in, and I can tell you, people are going to get hurt."

Richard hung up, but Luc still held the phone to his ear, the dial tone humming tonelessly. Mouth dry, heart pounding, he slowly, carefully replaced the receiver in its cradle.

"SO WHERE ARE WE headed?"

Good question.

Holly had been wondering that very thing for more than a week. Actually, almost since the moment she'd met Parker James. She never should have gone over to talk to him that first day. Never should have allowed herself to forget for even a second that nothing good could come of the two of them.

But she had, and now her heart was engaged and she couldn't undo any of it. Oh, she'd tried. Desperately. For the last several days, every time a thought of Parker rose up in her mind, she shut it down quickly. But it didn't seem to do any good. Whenever she slept, her brain was free to do as it pleased, and apparently it was determined to focus on Parker.

Her dreams were filled with him. And when she woke up alone, her heart ached.

"Hello?"

Holly heard the smile in Parker's voice.

"Want to give me a hint about where we're going?"

Holly slanted Parker a look, then turned her head to stare out the windshield again. Much easier to look at strangers, trees, traffic, than into those blue eyes of his.

"By Burke Park. Over on Annunciation."

"Huh."

"What?"

"Nothing," he said with a shrug. "It's just, that's the neighborhood I live in."

Perfect.

Instantly her back went up. "If you're thinking this is just another one of my nefarious 'plots' involving you, you can forget about it. I didn't know you lived there and—"

"Hey, hey, hey." He lifted one hand from the wheel briefly in mock surrender. "I didn't say anything. Just thought it was a coincidence. That's all."

"Fine."

"So what're we headed there for?"

To take a look at what could be Holly's future. Through friends of friends, she'd heard about an old house that was going up for sale soon. According to every report she'd had on it, the place needed a lot of work, but it was selling for much less than it would have otherwise. And her friend had gotten her the keys so she could look around.

In fact, it had felt too good to be true. Now that she'd learned Parker lived in the same area, she knew it was.

Still, she wouldn't allow him to ruin this for her.

"*I'm* going to look at a house," she said simply. "*You're* being a cabdriver."

"Right."

Holly folded her hands in her lap, linking her fingers together tightly. "Look, you said you wanted to talk to me, so talk."

Whatever he had to say to her, she would hear him out, then put it behind her. She wouldn't let him hurt her again. Wouldn't give him any more power to chip away at her heart.

He pulled up at a stoplight, tapped his fingers against the steering wheel and started talking.

"I've missed you, Holly."

She swallowed hard. Damn it. This wasn't fair. She didn't want to know that he missed her. Didn't want to start imagining that he had feelings for her. That would only make her nuts.

She cleared her throat and said, "You just saw me last night. At the hotel."

"From the back of the room."

Yes, but she'd seen him there. Felt his presence.

And she'd sung to him. She wondered if he'd known that. If he'd seen that her heart was in her song? Probably not.

She sighed heavily. "What is it you want from me, Parker?"

"Damned if I know," he murmured, and stepped on the gas, taking a left turn on Washington Avenue.

Holly looked out the window at Lafayette Cemetery Number One. Some of the trees were gone now after Hurricane Katrina, but the tombs, the monuments, were still standing as silent sentinels to the past. Instinctively she dipped her head in a small show of respect for those buried there.

As they passed Chestnut Street, Parker said, "My house is right down there."

Too close, she thought. Way too close for comfort. Even if she could swing buying this place…even if she made it her home, brought in the foster children she was determined to have…Parker would be practically around the corner.

Oh, God. How would she manage to live here and not think about him?

"I'm sorry," he said softly. "About our last night together. About what I said. What I thought."

She turned to look at his profile and forced herself to remember every awful accusation he'd hurled at her. If she could only find her rage again, that might be enough to protect her and keep her from acknowledging one very sad truth.

She loved him.

Holly winced, took a breath and held it. Yes, it was fast, but the simple truth was unavoidable. She loved his passion, loved his smile. She loved how he made her feel and, heaven help her, she even loved arguing with him. She hadn't wanted to look at her own feelings and see them for what they were. But ignoring them wouldn't make them go away.

She loved Parker James.

And she'd never have him.

Best to just get used to it now and learn to move on.

"Thanks," she said. "I appreciate the apology. Even though you've said that before."

"I've been thinking about that night, Holly. A lot."

"Me, too."

"And I need to know. Are you pregnant?"

She goggled at him for a second or two. *"That's* what this is about? This apology? This little ride together for a heart-to-heart chat?"

"No." His fists tightened on the steering wheel. "Well, not completely. Damn it, I've got a right to know if you're carrying my baby."

"Well, I'm not. At least, I don't know yet."

"When will you know?"

"A few days." She forced herself to keep looking at him. "But even if I am—" *God forbid* "—you don't have anything to worry about."

"Meaning…?"

"Meaning, I'll take care of the baby myself. I already told you I don't want anything from you, Parker. I don't know how to be more clear than that." She pointed. "That's Annunciation. Turn right."

"Holly, if you're pregnant, then we *both* take care of that baby."

"No thanks," she muttered. "My baby won't need a 'duty' daddy. There it is! Pull up here."

He parked and turned to look in the direction she'd indicated, but Holly barely noticed. All she could see was the house—and possibilities.

It was huge. Four chimneys, three stories and ironwork railings on the balconies. Faded pink paint was peeling from the sides of the house, and the weeds and grass were high enough to give an invading army plenty of cover. The windows were dirty and the surrounding trees looked like gnarled old men gathered for a bitching session.

"It's…" she said.

"It's…" he said.

"Perfect."

"Hideous."

"What do you know?" Holly demanded before opening her door and leaping out of the car. She was halfway across the street before Parker caught up to her. Taking her elbow in a firm grip, he refused to be shaken off. "Oh, look," she said. "The front porch is great. Wraps all the way around the house."

"Probably the only thing holding it up."

"The yard's so big, and those trees…"

"…look like they're going to topple over on top of the place."

"*Four* chimneys," she said dreamily, not even listening to Parker now, so caught up in a vision of children playing in the yard.

"Probably stuffed with birds' nests and squirrels."

"A bay window at the front of the house."

"Cracked."

She dug in her purse and came up with an old, tarnished brass key ring. "I'm going in."

"Are you nuts?"

Finally she stopped, yanked her arm free and whirled around to face him. "Why are you still here? You gave me a ride, you apologized. Again. Go away."

Frowning down at her, he said, "And leave you alone here? I don't think so."

"I don't need your help and I don't want you here."

"You've made that clear enough," he admitted. "But I'm still not letting you go strolling through this death trap on your own."

"It's not a death trap," she snapped. All the old house needed was someone to love it again. It needed to become a *home* again. To have laughter and shouts echoing through its rooms.

It was as if the old house was calling to her, asking her to rescue it from the silence.

And that's just what she was going to do.

"It's *mine*."

She hurried up the cracked sidewalk, stepped onto the porch and grinned at the sound of her heels on the worn boards. Turning the key in the lock, she opened the door and stepped into the shadowy cool.

"Holly."

She glanced back at him over her shoulder. Her excitement at finding this old jewel was only slightly marred by knowing that Parker would never be a part of her life. That they would never sit together in the big old living room and listen to the sounds of children clattering up and down the staircase.

But when she'd first conceived this dream, he hadn't been a part of it. The fact that he still wasn't didn't change anything, did it?

"Don't look so worried, Parker. I'm not crazy. I'm just *home*."

"Why would you want to buy this old place? It's huge, for one thing, and falling down for another."

"It can be fixed," she said, nodding as she walked through the main hall and stepped into the empty, cavernous living room. She ran one hand across the peeling paint on the wall and smiled as if looking at an original Gauguin. "It just needs to be loved."

"But why's it so important to you? Why this house? Why now?"

CHAPTER TWELVE

PARKER LISTENED to Holly talk as he followed her through the house. Her voice rang with excitement as she outlined her plans for a permanent home for foster children.

"Kids deserve homes, Parker," she said wistfully, her gaze moving over the walls, the scarred floors, the broken windows.

And he knew she was seeing the house as it could be, not as it was.

"I didn't have that," she said in a matter-of-fact voice belied by the pain in her eyes. "I never had the feeling that I belonged. That I mattered. As soon as I was old enough, I split. Went out on my own and made my own family."

"Holly…"

She shook her head and gave him a small smile. "Don't. That wasn't a bid for sympathy. It was a long time ago and I'm over it."

He didn't think so, but doubted she'd want to hear that at the moment.

"But the kids who are out there today, waiting, hoping that someone will want them…they matter."

Her voice was soft but firm, and he knew that no matter what she had to do, she would find a way to make other children's lives better.

While they walked through the house, he only half listened to her, thinking instead about the childhood she'd described so briefly. On her own at sixteen, she hadn't given up, but had made a life she could be proud of. And now she wanted to share that life with kids who might not have her tenacity and self-confidence. He admired her for it. For all of it.

And once again, he felt like the worst kind of ass for everything he'd said to her on their last night together. For insinuating that she was trying to use him to ensure herself an easy life.

Their footsteps echoed weirdly in the emptiness, but as Holly continued to describe, explaining her dream, her plans, the house began to change in Parker's mind.

He began to see it as she did. He could almost smell the fresh paint and see the sun glinting on the now dusty, hardwood floors. When he looked out the windows, he didn't see the years of grime caked on the glass, he saw sunbeams splintering through them to shine down on a well-tended lawn with a swing hanging from one of the tree branches. The house needed a lot of work, true. But in the end, it would be a special place.

She started up the stairs, mindlessly dragging her left hand along the filthy banister, her attention focused on the second-floor landing. "It's perfect. Or it will be," she said, as if convincing herself as well as Parker. "With a house this size, I can take in at least six kids. Maybe more."

"And who's with them when you work?"

She flashed him a grin. "I'll hire help. Maybe a nice grandmotherly type who can use a home to love as much as the kids."

"House is gonna need a lot of work."

She frowned. "I can see that. But it's going to be—"

"Perfect?" he finished for her.

Holly's smile took his breath away.

"You catch on quick," she said, then yelped as her right foot went right through one of the stair treads.

The old wood splintered as she fell, her leg sinking up to her knee. She wobbled, flung her arms out for balance, but Parker was too fast for her. He took the two steps separating them and caught her as she went down.

Heartbeat thundering, he cradled her against his chest, wrapping his arms around her and holding on. "You okay? God, Holly, are you hurt?"

"My foot hurts," she admitted, and tried to pull her leg free.

"Wait, wait," he ordered, right hand sliding down into the gaping hole and checking for breaks in her leg. "I think you're okay, but pull it out slowly, all right?"

"Right." Carefully, she did as he asked, and when her foot was free, she groaned.

"What? Are you in pain?"

"My *shoe*," she whined, and wiggled her bare toes as if to show him that she'd left something behind. "These shoes are brand-new and they cost a fortune and—"

"Oh, for God's sake," he muttered, choking back his worry. Still holding on to her, he reached down into the hole and fished around until he finally came up with a ridiculously flimsy-sandaled heel.

"Thanks," she said, and stood with his help. As soon as she put her weight on her foot, she yelped again and instantly lifted it up.

"It *is* hurt."

"Guess so."

"You're lucky you didn't break your neck."

"Born under a lucky star," she muttered. "That's me."

He swept her up into his arms and tightened his grip when she tried to wriggle loose. "Forget it. You're not walking down these stairs again."

"Down? No!" She made another futile attempt to escape. "I want to see the rest of the house."

"The rest of the house," Parker said, heading for the front door, "will most likely fall down on top of you."

"Parker, stop."

"Not a chance, Holly." His heart was still beating frantically at the thought of what could have happened if he hadn't been with her today. She could have been stuck in this damn house for hours. Days, even. His arms tightened around her until she squeaked in protest. "Sorry." He loosened his grip on her slightly. "But no way are you trooping through this place anymore today."

"Since when do you get to tell me what to do?"

"Since now. Deal with it."

"This may come as news to you, Parker, but I don't really go for the Tarzan kind of man."

"I'll make a note." He stepped onto the porch. "Close the door and lock it."

She did, muttering a stream of words that he figured he was better off not hearing. When she was finished, he carried her out to the street and settled her into the passenger seat of his car.

"I'm calling a cab, remember?"

"No, you're not. You're coming with me."

"Fine. Take me home then."

"I intend to. *My* home."

STILL SPUTTERING angrily, Holly glared at him on the short ride to his house. She didn't want his help. Okay, she might need it at the moment, but she didn't *want* it. But arguing with him was as pointless as trying to talk a tree into moving from one side of the lawn to the other.

So instead, she settled into sulky silence.

Even when he'd parked in front of a beautiful but small home on a wide, neatly tended lot, she refused to speak. Childish? Maybe. But it was the only weapon she had left.

He came around the car, opened her door and scooped her up again before she had a chance to slide out on her own.

"I'm capable of walking, you know."

"Your foot is hurt. Let's clean it up and check it out. See if you need a trip to the ER."

"The hospital?" She pushed away from the broad expanse of his chest, even though her instincts were to burrow closer. He was being high-handed and bossy, and a part of her was really enjoying it. Of course, she hated to admit it, but, oh, how she loved the feel of his arms around her. "I don't need a hospital, for heaven's sake."

"We'll find out in a minute or two."

He stalked up the flower-lined walk, crossed the porch and had the door unlocked and opened in a few minutes. When he carried her over the threshold, she tried not to think of it in just those terms. Impossible, though. She couldn't keep her mind from drifting in the direction it preferred. But she could do her best to combat it.

"Nice place," she said as he carried her down the hall and into a guest powder room. She didn't get to see much more of the house than the hall and a quick glimpse of the living room. But what she did see was neat and very plain. Cream-colored walls, brown couches, a few paintings adding a splash of color. The man clearly didn't put a lot of effort into decorating.

"Thanks." He set her gently on the sea-green granite countertop, stepped back and cradled her injured foot in his big hands.

Goose bumps raced along her flesh and she tried not to focus on the feel of his hands on her. But, Lordy, it wasn't easy.

"So, Doctor?" she quipped with a forced light-heartedness. "Will I live?"

"There's a bruise already blooming on the outside of your ankle," he said quietly, fingers tracing over her injured flesh. "Can you move your foot?"

"Of course I can—*ow!*"

One dark eyebrow lifted as he looked at her. "I don't think it's broken, but it's a good sprain."

Pain still shimmered along her nerve endings. "That's great. That's terrific. Won't I look gorgeous up on stage with a cane and my foot all wrapped up in some tasteful bandage?"

"Yeah," he said, running his hand up from her ankle, along her calf to the back of her knee. "You will."

At his touch, anticipation exploded inside her and Holly felt her body begin to hum. His fingertips were feather-light against her skin and every cell in her body ached for more. Oh, she wanted to touch him again. Wanted to feel his body along hers. Taking a deep breath, she swallowed hard before trusting herself to speak again.

"Parker…"

"Holly, I want you to know you…mean something to me," he said, and she could see that he was biting off every word as though forcing himself to say it.

Pain lanced through her, almost making her

groan out loud. He *cared*. What a pitifully shallow emotion. It cost a person nothing to care. There was no risk to the emotions. No reward. The feeling was tepid at best and warmed neither giver nor receiver.

Maybe someone else would have been satisfied with "you mean something to me." But not her. She'd been down this road before and she wasn't willing to travel it any farther this time.

Jeff had "cared" for her until she had wanted more. Now Parker was looking into her eyes and telling her pretty much the same thing. She wouldn't hang around long enough to watch him walk away.

"Parker…"

"I've missed seeing you," he said before she could go on. "I think about you. Hell, I *dream* about you. I'm not sure how I feel about that." He raked one hand impatiently through his hair. "But I wanted you to know."

"You wanted me to know that you 'care.'"

"Well, *yes*."

"God, Parker…" She swallowed hard past the knot of misery in her throat. How could she have set herself up for this yet again? How had she stumbled blindly into a situation that was as risky to her heart as the emotional minefield she'd survived three years before?

Worse, how could she have allowed herself to feel

so much more for this man? To let desire become affection? To let affection become *love?*

Regret swelled inside her. He cared, but didn't want to. He dreamed about her but didn't sound happy about it. While her emotions were like a raging inferno, his were barely lukewarm.

Shaking her head, she said softly, more to herself than to him, "I can't do this anymore."

"Do what?" he asked, gently releasing his hold on her foot.

"This." She waved both hands between them and looked him square in the eye. Oh, she'd be seeing those eyes of his in her dreams for years. The color of a cool, mountain lake, they held depths that she was willing to bet even he didn't know about.

And as she watched him, she knew just how deeply she loved him. Knew that every day without him was going to be a lonely one. Even walking away from him wouldn't spare her heart the pain that was already blossoming on her horizon.

"I can't, Parker. Seeing you, wanting you, fighting with you. I just can't do it. It hurts me." She fisted a hand and held it at her breast. "And if I stay, it'll destroy me."

He took a step back, his mouth working as if he were chewing on words that wanted to get out.

Finally, though, he said, "I'm not trying to hurt you, Holly. I'm only trying to be honest."

"I know that. I do. Really." She scooted off the edge of the counter and kept most of her weight on her good foot. It would have been easier to say what she had to say sitting, but she needed to be on her own two feet—well, one and a half feet.

He reached for her, but she lifted one hand to keep him at bay. If he touched her now, she'd shatter. "No, please don't touch me. I won't be able to think. Worse, I won't *want* to think."

"Holly…"

"Just let me talk."

Shoving both hands into his back pockets, he nodded and waited.

"God, this isn't easy." He looked lost, she thought. And worried. His eyes shone in the glare of the overhead light. Holly breathed in the homey scent of pine cleaning solution and knew that she would always associate that scent with this moment. This memory would be with her forever. She wished it could have been a happier one.

Hoping her thoughts and feelings would meld together and become the words she wanted— *needed*—to say, she started talking and hoped for the best. "You say I mean something to you—"

"You do."

"That's not enough, Parker."

He looked down and his dark hair fell across his forehead. It was all she could do not to reach out and brush it back.

"Holly, I don't know if I can give you anything more," he said, focusing on her once again.

Regret shone in his eyes and she wanted to weep. He couldn't give her what she wanted from him. And if she hung around waiting, hoping, she'd only end up more wounded than she had been when Jeff had left her.

She had thought, three years ago, that the pain engulfing her couldn't have gone any deeper. Now she knew she had been wrong. This pain was so much more…because what she was feeling was so much more.

Like the sun bursting out from behind a bank of gray storm clouds, the truth shone down on her, and it amazed her that she hadn't recognized it sooner. But then, maybe she hadn't wanted to. Maybe it had been easier to pretend differently.

But in the end, the truth was all she had. And better to face it now than later.

"You can't give me more, and I can't settle for less," she said with a small shrug. "You see, Parker, I don't just care for you. I love you."

Parker backed up until he was flat against the bathroom wall. If he'd had room, Holly was sure he would have bolted. She buried the hurt inside her, unwilling to let him see just how close to tears she really was.

"I—"

"Don't, okay?" She found a smile somewhere and plastered it on her face. It felt false, almost painful, but she kept it there with determination. "Don't say you're sorry, or you wish things were different. It won't change anything."

"Damn it, Holly," he said tightly, "I didn't mean for this to happen."

"Neither did I, Parker. But it did, and if it's okay by you, I'll just deal with this by myself. I don't need you to hold my hand. I don't need you worrying about me. Eventually, I'll be fine."

God, please let her be fine. Please let the pain that was twisting her stomach into knots ease away day by day. Please let her find her balance again. Let her enjoy her life the way it was before Parker had wandered into it.

"If you'll just let me call a cab," she said, "I'll get out of your hair and we can each move on with our life. Forget all about this."

"I won't forget you," he said, his voice tearing

from him like a groan. "Wouldn't be able to even if I tried."

She forced a smile. "See? There you go, saying something nice that doesn't change a thing."

"Holly—"

"*Please,* Parker," she interrupted quickly, desperate now to escape with what little dignity she had left. "If I mean anything to you at all, you'll just let me get a cab and go home."

His blue eyes fixed on her as though he were trying to read her mind, her soul. But everything she was had already been laid out in the open for him. She still saw regret in his eyes and knew that if she didn't get out of that house and into the comfort of her own space soon, she was going to embarrass them both by wailing.

"I'll take you home."

"I'd rather not—"

"I said," Parker repeated flatly, with absolutely no hint as to what he was feeling, "I'll take you home."

He wasn't going to budge, Holly knew. The man had *stubborn* written all over his face. And in the end, did it really make a difference how she got home?

"Fine." Maybe he needed to play the gentleman to the last—and if so, she'd agree. Anything, she thought. Anything to get her out of his house and away from his blue eyes, so full of what-might-have-beens.

PARKER STAYED AWAY from the Hotel Marchand for the next few days. Instead he burrowed into his office at the jazz café and worked hard to forget about Holly.

I love you.

He threw his pen down on top of the inventory sheet and leaned back in his chair, staring at the ceiling.

I love you.

He heard Holly's voice over and over again in his mind. He saw her eyes and the small flash of pain dulling the gray when he couldn't say what she so wanted to hear.

I love you.

"God."

He'd like to believe that she was telling him the truth. To believe that love—real love—could happen so quickly. He'd like to believe that Holly meant what she said. That she looked at him and saw a man she wanted to spend her life with.

But how the hell could he?

"No," he said out loud, more because he needed to hear the sound of his own voice in the suffocating silence than for any other reason. "I won't risk it again. I can't."

Sighing, he sat up and reached for his pen again. Maybe this time he could forget about Holly by losing himself in work.

HOLLY TOOK some time off.

She used her sprained ankle as an excuse and it worked well with Tommy, who didn't question her. But she knew the truth. She knew that she was hiding. But she simply couldn't bring herself to face Parker again. Not yet, anyway.

Especially not *now*.

"God really does have a sense of humor," she whispered as she looked down at the plastic stick in her hand.

The plus sign was unmistakable.

She set it down on the bathroom counter, right beside the three other sticks, all displaying the same result.

"Pregnant."

What was she supposed to do now? Should she tell Parker? Didn't he have a right to know? Or would the knowledge of this baby only make things worse? He'd already made it clear he didn't want Holly in his life. Why should he want her child?

Her heart started to pound and a ball of nerves skittered uneasily in the pit of her stomach.

Her child.

She was going to be a mother.

At last, she would have a family of her own.

Someone to love. Someone to love her back.

Someone to build dreams around.

She and her child would live in that great old house and expand their family, welcoming other children, building lives that would be full and rich—everything she used to dream of.

Staring into the mirror, she saw the worry and excitement tangling together in her own eyes. Funny, she'd spent so much energy hoping she wasn't pregnant that she hadn't for a moment considered how wonderful it would be to find out she *was*.

Her hands dropped to her flat belly and rested protectively there, as if she could somehow soothe the tiny child within. It'll be okay, she thought. We'll be okay. You'll see.

She took a long, deep breath and slowly, so very slowly, found a smile. Her baby's father might want to disappear from her life—but she would have her child.

Always.

When the doorbell rang, a quick jolt of hope rose up inside her in spite of everything. Maybe it was Parker. Maybe he had come to his senses and realized that the love she offered him was a gift, not a trap.

She swept the pregnancy tests into the trash can and gave her hair a quick check in the mirror, then turned and hurried as best she could to the front door.

She opened the door to find the last person she was expecting to see.

"Ah. The little jazz singer," Frannie LeBourdais purred as she blithely blew past Holly to stalk into the living room. "It's time we had a little talk."

CHAPTER THIRTEEN

FRANNIE DROPPED HER crocodile bag and a manila folder onto the magazine-strewn coffee table and let her gaze slide around the small room. Overstuffed furniture, tacky little knickknacks and a view out the front window of a yard that needed landscaping.

Not very impressive, but it cheered her immensely.

"What are you doing here?" Holly demanded.

"Why, Holly—you don't mind if I call you Holly, do you?" Frannie asked, carefully lowering herself to sit on the edge of a sofa cushion. "After all, we've known each other a very long time."

Holly walked across the room, limping slightly. "I'm sorry?"

"Oh." Frannie waved one hand to dismiss that statement. "Now, this is just between us girls, so let's be frank, shall we? I remember you. You sang at my wedding."

"Yes."

"And we met the night *before* the wedding, as well." Just recalling that moment filled Frannie with a fury she was hard-pressed to tamp down.

Once she had received a complete file from her private investigator, she'd remembered everything. How she and Justine had been discovered by a nobody singer. Frannie had worried that the little bitch would spill the truth to Parker and ruin a match she had wanted very much.

Odd that now, ten years later, the same little bitch was still a thorn in Frannie's side. And the threat she represented was still very real. If Holly Carlyle were to tell Parker about her indiscretions, Frannie wouldn't have a chance in hell of winning back her husband.

Well, enough was enough. She'd get rid of this woman—finally—and move on.

"That was a long time ago," Holly said.

"Yes, it was," Frannie agreed, standing. Damned if she'd look up at the other woman. "And yet, here we are."

"What I'm wondering is, why you're here."

"Easily answered," Frannie said, sliding the folder out from under her bag. She watched Holly speculatively. "I've actually come to bring you a message from Parker."

"Parker?"

"My husband?" Frannie prompted unnecessarily. Oh, this was more fun than she'd expected. Allowing a small smile to tug at the corners of her mouth, she continued. "You remember? The man you were having sex with?"

Holly winced.

"He doesn't want to see you anymore."

She flinched, but stood her ground, and Frannie had to admire her just a little. Not that it changed a thing.

"He sent you here?"

"Certainly," she lied. "You don't think Parker would bother himself with these little details, do you?"

"I don't believe you."

"Oh, I think you do." Frannie handed her the file, walked to the front window and then turned around to face her again. "In some part of you, you know that Parker never really took you seriously. You had to realize that a man like him would look at you as...a distraction. You see, Parker and I have an 'arrangement.' Our marriage is more...fluid than most. We find other...companionship...where we choose, but we never lose sight of the fact that we're married."

"Strange." Holly gripped the folder tightly, but didn't look inside. She swayed slightly on her feet, as if her world was rocking, and Frannie was forced to hide another small smile of victory. "If your marriage is so sound, I wonder why the reports of your upcoming divorce are such big news?"

"Please. No one believes what they read in the newspapers." Checking the polish on her nails, she added, "I admit, after our last disagreement, Parker was a bit hasty and spoke to a lawyer, but that's all going to be sorted out."

"Uh-huh."

"As for my preference for female lovers, Parker knows all about that." A lie, but a good one. How would Holly know it wasn't the truth? No reason for her to go crying off to Parker if she thought he already knew. "So Parker wanted you to know that there's no reason to go running off to him, trying to salvage what's left of your 'relationship.'"

"I see. And why is it Parker sent you to me?"

"Oh, Holly." Frannie clucked her tongue and shook her head sadly. "Do you really think he wanted to involve himself in what could possibly become a very embarrassing scene?"

No, he wouldn't, Holly realized. She remembered the strain on his face when she'd proclaimed her love. Remembered with perfect clarity that he'd looked as though he would rather be anywhere else at that particular moment. Holly fought against acknowledging the pain that memory brought to her.

What would he think, she wondered, if he knew about the coming baby? Would he be horrified? Sad? God, she would never know.

"And what's this?" Holly lifted the file, inwardly pleased that her hand didn't shake.

"Take a look," Frannie invited her.

She did. Opening the folder, she flipped through the pages tucked inside and felt a chill sweep over her. Someone had looked into her background. Peered into the shadows of her life and laid her mistakes out for Frannie to pore over.

But was it just Frannie? Had Parker read the report on her life? Had they laughed together over a woman like her professing to love him?

Hurt and fury constricted her chest and made breathing a real challenge. Was this his answer to being loved? Had he really sent his wife here to tell her to go away? Did he think so little of her? Of what they'd shared so briefly? "Did Parker do this? Did he have me investigated?"

"Actually, I did."

"You?"

"My dear." The tall, elegant woman laughed shortly and bent to snatch up her purse from the coffee table. "You should know that I will do whatever is necessary to protect my marriage. To keep what is mine. At the moment, Parker is still thinking of you fondly—however misguided those feelings may be. You see, he hasn't yet seen these papers."

Relief, sweet and sharp, slapped at Holly. At least she had this much. He hadn't stooped to digging into a past that had nothing to do with him.

"But," Frannie added, "should you dare approach my husband again, you can be sure I'll give him a copy of those reports."

"Why would you bother? If Parker is over me, as you say, what's there to worry about?"

"Oh, if I've given you the impression that you actually *worry* me, then you're mistaken." Frannie looked at her with a sympathetic smirk. "This file is only…insurance. In case he should change his mind and approach you again. Should that happen, I'll see that he receives a copy of these files. I'll make certain that he knows you for exactly what you are. A pitiful, social-climbing, money-grabber with no more thought for Parker than you would have for any other man who is too good for you."

"He won't believe you."

"Oh, I think he will." Frannie gave her another smile. "But there's more. If you don't stay clear of Parker, I'll see to it that this file is sent to Social Services."

Holly inhaled sharply.

"I see you understand me. I'm sure the state of Louisiana would consider your past unsavory enough to keep you from your dream of being a foster parent."

"They're juvenile records," Holly muttered. "Sealed. How did you—and how did you know about my plans?"

"My investigator is very thorough. You've taken classes. You've already started the necessary paperwork." Frannie gave her a cold stare. "And I can end it all."

She could. Holly's juvenile record was sealed and shouldn't have been a problem with the state. But if Frannie made good on her threat...

"Blackmail?"

"Such an ugly word." Frannie looked as if she had just sniffed something unpleasant. "Accurate, but ugly."

"Why are you doing this?" Holly hated the desperation she heard in her voice.

"My goodness, you *are* dim, aren't you?" Frannie shook her head. "No matter. I believe I've been quite clear on that score, but allow me to elaborate once again. You're nothing to me, Ms. Carlyle. Less than nothing. But should you become a bigger irritant than you already are, I shall take whatever steps I have to to rid myself of you."

"An awful lot of bother for someone who's less than nothing."

She smiled. "I'm certain Parker would find your file very entertaining reading, if that's any consolation. Discovering that you spent time in juvenile hall for shoplifting—not to mention the arrest for public nudity... Really, a less than stellar résumé for someone who wants to care for foster children."

Okay, now the anger churning inside her overtook the misery and disappointment. Holly wouldn't have her past dragged out and examined by anyone. And she for damn sure wasn't going to stand still to be insulted in her own living room. She might have been shocked into silence before, but that was over now and she was more than willing to fight back. "I was a kid. And hungry. I 'shoplifted' a loaf of bread."

"Very sad, I'm sure. Practically Dickensian."

"And the public nudity charge—" Holly slapped one hand against the incriminating file. "I flashed my breasts for a string of beads on Mardi Gras—just like every other woman in New Orleans. It means *nothing*."

"You poor thing. You actually believe that, don't you?" Frannie sighed then tucked her envelope under her left arm. "You've entered a battle completely unarmed. Your background is ridiculous. Your present isn't much better. A singer with questionable morals trying to sleep her way to respectability? I don't think so. You couldn't possibly have thought that a *slut* could worm her way into the James family."

Holly flushed with a red-hot surge of fury that nearly blinded her as she stared at the so-composed woman opposite her. No wonder Parker didn't want to hear anything about "love." Holly was ready to slug this woman after only ten minutes, and he'd spent ten years married to her! If that hadn't scarred Parker, it would be a miracle. To get her own way, Frannie was prepared to shatter Holly's life. Not only would she lose Parker, she could lose the dream she'd been nurturing for years.

Her hands fisted on the file folder holding the more embarrassing moments of her life and she looked into a pair of icy-blue eyes.

Nothing was going to touch this woman. No insult. No warmth. Nothing.

And yet she heard herself strike back, anyway. "Sluts aren't welcome but lesbians are?"

Frannie flinched but quickly regained her composure. "Ah, a street cat, trying to swipe her claws at a target far too high for her. Pitiable, but certainly understandable."

Holly clenched her back teeth so tightly, she wouldn't have been surprised to find they'd turned to powder. "You've delivered your message. And your threats. I think it's time you left."

"I'll be leaving soon. There's just one more bit of business we need to clear up."

"What else could you possibly have to say that concerns me?"

"Your dreams." Frannie's voice was now falsely soothing, and Holly went on full alert.

"What are you talking about?"

"I know all about your dreams, Holly. You want to buy that monstrosity of a house on Annunciation for an underprivileged litter of kiddies."

Holly glared at the woman. "What about it?"

"I can help make that possible."

"Why would you?"

"Call it a gift for favors done."

"What favors?" God, she couldn't even believe she was asking that question. Morbid curiosity? This must be what striking a deal with the devil felt like.

"You stay away from Parker, even if he comes crawling back, you help me regain the affections of my husband," Frannie said slyly, "and I will buy that house outright and hand it to you."

Stunned, Holly just stared at her. She couldn't believe this whole conversation. The woman had gone from extortion to bribery in the blink of an eye.

That one fact made her realize the desperation buried beneath Frannie's cool sophistication. Maybe Frannie was telling the truth about Parker—maybe not. But if nothing else, this uncomfortable little visit had underscored what Holly already knew.

She and Parker might as well be on two different planets.

Parker had allowed this vicious woman to ruin his chances for a life with someone who truly loved him. Holly had started out with nothing, but she wouldn't let anyone stop her from realizing her dreams.

Knowing that gave her the courage to tell Frannie exactly what she thought of her offer.

"Take your file and your private investigator and get out of my life." Holly sneered at her. "I can't be bought. Or paid off. Or blackmailed. Do what you want with this 'information' you've gathered. I'm not ashamed of who I am. And I don't care who you tell."

"You really are a stupid girl, aren't you?"

"Just leave. I'm not interested in playing your games."

Frannie's eyes darkened.

"You can't hurt me," Holly said, and walked to the front door. Turning the knob, she threw the door open and stood there like a sentinel. "So do whatever you want with the information you've scrounged. Do your worst. As far as I'm concerned, you don't even exist. So if you don't mind, I'd like you to leave my house now."

She could almost see the steam coming off the top of Frannie's head. Apparently the ice queen actually did have a temper, after all.

With a few long strides, Frannie reached the door. She stopped to look Holly up and down dismissively. "You were no more than a blip on my radar, Holly. And now? You're not even that. I tried to help you, but some people simply don't know a good thing when they hear it."

Holly's fingers tightened on the door. "You're still here."

With an indignant huff, Frannie stalked from the apartment. Holly shut the door quietly behind her. Throwing the lock, she braced her back on the door and slowly slid to the floor. Pulling her knees up to her chest, she wrapped her arms around them, dropped her head on her knees and cried.

For Parker.

For herself.

For the baby he would never know.

PARKER'S DREAMS tortured him.

Holly rose over him, her fingers trailing down his naked chest. Eyes closed, he saw her as she had been the last time they were together. Hair wild and loose, eyes flashing, mouth curved in a smile that was both sensuous and innocent.

He wanted her desperately. And even though he knew he was dreaming, he forced himself to stay in that foggy half sleep that would keep Holly in his arms forever.

"Holly…" The whispered word was like a prayerful sigh.

Lips on his, soft, demanding. Her scent filled him—but it was all wrong. Too thick. Too harsh.

His eyes flew open and he stared up at Frannie. Her hands were at his shoulders, and she straddled him, naked, a pleased smile on her face.

He blinked at her a couple dozen times and tried to bring his mind into focus. To drag himself out of the dream and into the all-too-real world. Once he had, he pushed her off him, jumped out of bed and stared at her as if he'd never seen her before.

"What the hell are you doing? How did you get in here? Why?"

Sighing, she said, "You're a creature of habit, Parker. You still keep a spare key in the flower bed on the right side of the porch." Frannie pouted as she stretched out in his bed, laid her head on the pillow and smoothed both of her hands up and down her shapely body. "Now, is that any way to talk to your wife?"

"What're you playing at Frannie?" He hurled the question at her while he reached for the robe he'd left at the end of the bed. He tugged it on, then yanked the sheets over the naked woman in his bed.

Once upon a time, he'd looked at her as she was now and felt desire. A quickening he'd hoped would contribute to making their life together a good one. Now all he felt was disgust. He wanted nothing more than to go take a shower. First, though, he had to get her the hell out of his house.

She clutched the sheet to her and sat up, tossing her hair back from her face. "I can remember a time when you weren't so eager to get out of our bed, Parker."

"Too long ago to think about, Frannie. What the hell are you up to?"

"Fine," she snapped, thrusting the sheet aside and rising. She walked slowly to the chair in the corner of his bedroom, where she'd tossed her clothes after sneaking into his room.

Note to self: change the locks.

"Only woman you want now is that cheap little redhead, is that it?"

A surge of protectiveness welled up in him. "What do you know about Holly?"

She laughed, but the sound had no music to it. No warmth. "A lot more than you, I'm willing to wager."

"If you've got something to say, say it and get out."

She whirled around, fingers buttoning up her silk blouse and then pulling up her skirt and zipping it closed. "Oh, I've got plenty to say. You want to throw me aside for that little bitch? Well, let me just fill you in on a few things, Parker, *honey.*"

She talked, her voice spitting out information, dates, places, times. She described every piece of information her private detective had turned up about Holly's past, and as she talked, Parker felt...*what?* He couldn't be angry that Holly hadn't told him. Neither of them had talked much about their past, but he knew enough about her childhood to understand she had done what she'd had to do to survive.

When Frannie wound down, she delivered the final salvo that cut his legs out from under him.

"The funniest part, Parker?" she taunted as she snatched up her purse and headed for the bedroom door. "I wanted you back. I wanted to make our marriage work. So I offered her cash to leave you the hell alone. Told her I'd buy her that damn house she wants so badly if she'd just turn her back on you." Her smile was triumphant. "And you know what, honey? Your little tramp took the money."

Parker's world rocked.

"That's right." Frannie smiled serenely, clearly enjoying herself. "She latched right on to my bribe. Took the money for that dump almost before I could get the offer out of my mouth. So," she added thoughtfully, "if you're tossing me aside to make room for her in your life, you're fresh outta luck, sweetie. She made her choice. She threw you over for a broken-down old building and a half-baked dream. Now, how's *that* make you feel, honey?"

Parker watched her go, but hardly noticed, really. It was hard to concentrate on what was going on around you when the thing you feared most might just turn out to be true.

Damn it.

Rage and disappointment crowded together in his guts. Only one thing kept him from giving in to despair completely: Frannie was a liar. But even acknowledging that, he had to ask himself if Holly really had only been interested in him for his money.

And the pain of that possibility crippled him.

CHAPTER FOURTEEN

DAYS LATER, and Parker still couldn't get that last conversation with Frannie out of his mind.

Hell, what right did he have to be doubting Holly? Wasn't he the one who'd pulled back? When Holly had told him she loved him, wasn't he the one who had practically scrambled away from her? Away from the risk? The danger?

So why was he so damned torn to find out that none of it had been real? Shouldn't he have been happy to know that she was willing to be bought off and walk away from him without a second thought?

Sitting in his car outside the ramshackle old house Holly had taken him to only a week ago, he stared at the sold sign hanging on the front gate.

His last hope had been that Frannie had lied. But here was the proof. The house was sold. Holly had made her choice, and clearly, her "love" for him had been as nebulous as the promises Frannie had once made to him.

Slapping one hand against the steering wheel, he told himself he should be glad. Should be happy as hell he'd escaped unscathed. But the problem was, he hadn't. He was hurt. His heart was more battered now than it had been when his marriage had dissolved.

His jaw tight, his gaze furious behind his dark glasses, Parker knew he'd never be able to put all this behind him until he talked to Holly face-to-face.

"And by God," he whispered, "she's going to have to look me in the eye and admit that it was all a lie."

He threw the car into gear and stomped on the gas pedal. It was Friday, which meant she'd be singing at the Hotel Marchand tonight. He could wait a few hours. But when she took her break, he'd be talking to her in her dressing room. Didn't matter if her personal guard was there or not.

Nobody was going to keep him from talking to Holly tonight.

"GIRL," TOMMY SAID as he walked Holly to her dressing room for a mid-set break, "you sure you're feeling well enough to do another set?"

"I'm fine, honest." She forced a smile she knew he needed and took a long, deep breath. "I'm not sleeping very well, is all. I just need to sit for a bit, then I'll be raring to go again."

"I don't like this."

"I know."

Tommy and Shana both had been at their wit's end since she'd told them about the baby a few days ago. But once the shock had passed, they'd rallied to her side, just as they always had. The two people in the world Holly knew she could count on had come through for her again.

"You know I'm no big fan of Parker James," Tommy said, seeing her into her dressing room and watching while she sat. "Still think it was a big mistake to get involved with his kind in the first place."

"His kind?" she asked, smiling.

"You know what I mean. He's rich. Born rich. They've got different ways of looking at things, Holly. Different ideas on how things should be."

"He's not like that," she said, though her heart wasn't really convinced.

Maybe Parker *was* the kind of man Tommy believed him to be. He'd shut her out the minute she'd admitted to loving him. He'd sent his estranged wife over to her home to scare—or buy—her off. What kind of man would do that?

Certainly not the man she'd thought she had known.

"Doesn't really matter one way or the other," Tommy said quietly. "My point is, whatever the hell kind of man he is, he's got a right to know about his child."

"Tommy—"

"I mean it, little girl. A man's going to be a father, he's got a right to be panicky about it." He cupped her cheek in his palm and looked down into her eyes with love that surrounded Holly like a warm blanket on a cold night. "He might do nothing. Might not give a good damn, and if he doesn't, then he's even worse a man than I believed him to be."

She sighed.

"But…" Tommy insisted, "he's got the right to know. And you've got the obligation to tell him."

"I'll think about it. I promise."

He nodded slowly and straightened. "That's the best I can ask for right now, so I'll take it." He turned toward the door. "Now you sit and rest for a while. I'll have Leo send you some tea."

FIVE MINUTES LATER Holly sipped at her tea and thought about what Tommy had said. Maybe she did owe Parker the truth. If nothing else, she could thank him for the child she already loved desperately.

Then she could truly move on with her life.

Her stomach did a quick spin and lurch, and she took another slow sip of tea. The moment she'd realized she was pregnant, her stomach seemed to have turned on her. Not just morning sickness, this was all-day nausea. A constant reminder that her life was changing. That nothing would ever be the same again.

And she was grateful.

Amazing, really, how different a baby no bigger than a grain of rice could make a person feel. The skies looked bluer, the future looked richer and the present, despite the pain of Parker's loss, was filled with possibilities.

Parker.

She stared into the mirror over her dressing table and whispered, "It's okay, baby. We'll be fine. You'll see. I promise I will love you so much you won't even miss having a daddy."

Swallowing hard, she ran a brush through her hair and checked her makeup. She only had fifteen minutes left on her break and she had to be ready for her second set.

When a knock sounded at the door, she assumed it was Tommy and called, "Come on in."

In the mirror, her gaze locked with Parker's as he stepped into the room and stopped. Over his shoulder, she glimpsed Tommy's concerned expression before Parker closed the door quietly.

How could she be both happy to see him and so furious she wanted to kick him?

"Parker." Just saying his name again sounded bittersweet. "What're you doing here?"

"We need to talk."

"I don't think so." She spun around on her chair and looked up at him. "I think we're all real clear on where we stand."

"I need to hear it from you." He practically ground out the words.

"And why should I care about what you need?"

"Damn it, Holly—"

"Don't you curse at me, either," she snapped, and stood. If the world at the edges of her vision went a little wobbly, she wouldn't let him know it. "Blast you, Parker. If you didn't want me in your life, all you had to do was say so. You think I couldn't see for myself that you weren't interested in me saying *I love you?* You think I didn't see the panic in your eyes?"

"Still can't believe you bothered to say it," he muttered.

"Well, I'm kicking myself for it now, trust me," she pointed out.

"That's what it all boils down to, isn't it?" he asked wryly. *"Trust."*

"Ha!" Setting her iced tea down on the table behind her, she glared up at Parker and again fought the urge to kick him. "You're talking to me about *trust?*"

"Don't see why you're so mad. You got everything you ever wanted, didn't you?"

"You don't see why I'm *mad?*" Her voice hit a note she was pretty sure only dogs would be able to hear, but she couldn't seem to stop herself from shrieking.

"What the hell are you yelling about?" he demanded.

"Your amazing gall, that's what." Holly paced three quick steps before turning in the closet-size room and walking back to stop in front of him. "You speak to me of trust when you send your bitch of a wife to my home? To my *home?*"

"What?" His brows pulled together and pure confusion was etched into his features.

It was, Holly thought, a damn good act. If she hadn't already known the truth, he might have convinced her. But she did know and she didn't have a problem reminding him what had happened.

"She hired a detective, Parker. She paid a stranger to dig into my life. To turn it over and give it a good shake." The thought of Frannie discussing her life with Parker was unbearable. "Did you two have a good laugh over it? Did you enjoy reading about me being arrested? Make you feel superior? Well, I make no apologies for my past, Parker. Not to you. Not to any of your rich friends, either."

"Yeah?" He countered, grabbing her hand and holding on to it. "You think I give a good damn about you being arrested on Mardi Gras? Or when you were a kid? I don't. So how about an apology from you for selling me out to Frannie? Feel up to that?"

"What're you talking about?"

"She told me." He let her go, shook his head and stared at her as if he'd never seen her before. "She told me all of it. How she offered to buy you that big old house if you'd just stay away from me. And she told me just how fast you accepted the offer."

"That's crazy." Confusion rippled through her. What was going on?

"Is it?" he demanded. "I told myself she was lying until I went by the house today. There's a big sold sign hanging on the gate."

"Of course there is," Holly snapped. "I just bought it."

"And all you had to do to get it was sell me out. If you needed money that badly, you should have asked me. There was no need for all the romance. No need to deal with Frannie."

He looked as cold as his soon-to-be ex-wife. His eyes were frosty and his tone was harsh. Was he hurt? Or just angry? Hard to tell.

"You're crazy," Holly said flatly. "I told you before, I never wanted your money. I didn't want anything from you."

"But you were willing to take money from Frannie?"

"I wouldn't take a glass of water from that woman if I was on fire in the pits of hell," Holly said hotly. Spinning around, she rummaged through the stuff piled on the only other chair in the little room until she came up with her purse. Rummaging inside it, she finally found her checkbook, flipped it open and thrust it at him. "Here. Look for yourself. I wrote a check to the escrow company myself yesterday."

He took it, studied the neat figures written in black ink for a long moment, then looked at her again. "I don't understand."

"I'm getting that. Take a good look at the balance left. I used almost every dime I had to buy that house," she snapped. "You think I'm so small I'd take a bribe from a woman I wouldn't trust to tell me the time of day? You think I would sell myself, my *body*, for a chance at your bank account?"

She stuffed the checkbook back into her purse. When she spoke, her voice was cold. "Well, let me tell you something, Parker. I don't need you. And I don't whore myself for anyone or anything. I've worked like a dog for the last ten years, saving every penny I could round up. I've got a down payment on that house. Barely. But I did it myself. I didn't need your money, Parker." All of the air left her body in a rush. "I thought I just needed you."

He looked into her eyes for a long minute before finally whispering, "You're telling the truth, aren't you?"

She smiled wistfully. "I'm surprised you recognize it."

"God," he muttered, shoving both hands through his hair. "I'm an idiot."

"You'll get no argument from me."

Parker wiped one hand across his face and looked as miserable as a man could be. Shoulders slumped, he thrust both hands into his pants' pockets and braced his feet wide apart.

"I kept pulling back from you, Holly," he admitted. "Every time you got a little too close, I shut down. Told myself to keep my heart out of it. To enjoy what we had but not look for anything more."

"I know that," she whispered, heart breaking. "What I don't know is why."

"Because I'm an idiot," he said, sounding confused. "All I knew for sure was that Frannie and I made each other miserable. I wasn't interested in getting that involved again. I wanted to avoid feeling too much—to risk the kind of hurt and disappointment I'd already lived with."

"Oh, Parker," Holly said, reaching out one hand to lay it against his chest. Beneath her palm, she felt the strong, sure beat of his heart and knew that it was finally time to tell him the truth. To tell him what she'd seen the night before his marriage.

"You know," she said softly, "I've wondered over the years if I shouldn't have told you this before you married Frannie. Maybe things would have been different for you."

"Told me what?" Confusion clouded in his eyes.

She took a breath and said, "The night before your wedding, I showed up at the reception hall to drop off my music and to—" She waved one hand in the air and admitted "—doesn't matter why I was there. The point is that I wasn't alone."

"What're you trying to say?"

"I walked in on Frannie and her lover—making love on a tabletop."

Parker blinked. "Her lover? She was with someone the night before we got married?" He gave a
harsh laugh. "Well, hell. That explains a lot, doesn't
it? She had no intention of trying to make the marriage work, did she?" Shaking his head as if to clear
his brain, he demanded, "Who was he?"

"Wasn't a *he* at all, Parker," Holly told him with
a wince. "Frannie was with her maid of honor. Justine DuBois."

"Justine?" He didn't look as surprised as Holly
thought he might. "I never knew…I should have, I
guess. All those shopping trips they used to take
together. The long phone calls. The whispered conversations."

"Parker, you were willing to give your marriage
a try, to make it work," she reminded him. "It's not
your fault that you were with a woman who could
never love you the way you wanted her to."

"Why'd she even go through with it?" he muttered, more to himself than to her. "Was it just for the
money? The prestige?"

"I don't know," Holly said. "Maybe she doesn't
even know."

"Man, I feel like an idiot," he said, a rueful smile
on his face.

"Maybe I should have told you back then," she admitted.

"Water under a broken bridge, Holly." He shrugged. "Besides, I might not have believed you. Back then, I was convinced that Frannie and I could make a go of it."

Pulling his hands from his pockets, Parker cupped her face between his palms.

"But I'm not that man anymore. I'm seeing things clearly now. Maybe for the first time in my life. I'm so sorry, Holly," he whispered, hoping to make her see all that he was feeling. All that he was now no longer hesitant to share. And dear God, he prayed that he wasn't too late. That he hadn't lost the chance at something amazing because of his own fears.

"It's hard to admit," he said, "but I was scared by all you were making me feel. You opened up a need in me I didn't even know I had, but I was too leery to risk doing anything about it."

She reached up and covered his hands with hers. Tears glimmered in her warm, gray eyes, but didn't fall. "Parker, I felt the same way. I didn't want to care because I couldn't believe that you would ever really want me in your life."

"God, Holly…"

"And when you pulled away that last time, I knew

it was because you realized I would never fit into your world." Before he could protest, she hurried on. "I'm a nobody, Parker. I know that. In New Orleans society, you're a king and I'm a peasant." A smile twitched at her mouth. "Not that I mind being a peasant. I think it sounds a lot more fun than being a queen. But I don't have the kind of pedigree a man like you needs in a woman."

Parker laughed and shook his head. "We *are* a perfect match, Holly. You're an idiot, too."

"I beg your pardon?"

He grabbed her close, gave her a hug fit to break her ribs, then pulled back and kissed her until both of them were breathless.

"Don't you get it? Holly, if I want a damn pedigree, I'll go to the American Kennel Club. I want *you.* I think I always knew on some level that you were the one woman I was born to love. It was only my own fears that kept me from saying so."

"Parker…"

"I *love* you, Holly. Completely. Desperately. I love you so much, I'm going to spend the rest of my life proving that to you."

She gulped. "What do you—"

"I'm asking you to marry me, Holly. Just as soon

as Frannie's out of my life forever, I want to start a new life. With you."

Her mouth opened and closed a few times, but nothing came out and Parker laughed again.

"Who knew I could actually make you speechless?"

Shaking her head, she managed to say, "I do love you. Know that. Believe that."

"I do."

"But, Parker…"

"No buts."

"This is a big one, so think about it before you answer."

"Okay," he said, still not letting go of her. Not daring to let her out of his reach now that he finally had the chance to keep her in his life forever.

"If I marry you, I'll still want to live in that big ol' house I just bought. I'll still want to take in foster kids. That dream won't change."

"It doesn't have to," he promised, already loving the image of a house full of kids. "We'll get contractors out to start on the house as soon as escrow closes. And the minute we're married, we'll sign up for the foster program and we'll take in as many kids as they'll allow—though I warn you going in, I'm going to want one or two of our own kids, too."

She smiled up at him, and Parker felt as though

he'd just climbed the highest mountain and was taking in a breathtaking view.

"Just—please." He dipped his head, kissed her again. "Say you'll marry me."

"I'll never be the high-society wife you might need, Parker James," Holly said, leaning into him and cuddling close. "But I swear to you, I will love you forever."

"Honey, all I'll ever need is my jazz singer. You're the only world I'm interested in."

She pulled back and smiled up at him. "And the big house."

"And the big house."

"And the dog."

"A dog?" He grinned. "Deal."

"And the foster kids."

"And the foster kids." Parker dropped a kiss on her forehead.

"Plus the one we've already got cookin'."

"Plus the one—" Parker stopped. He felt his jaw drop. He looked into her eyes and saw the deep well of love and pride and joy shining back at him. "You're pregnant?"

"I am," she said, taking one of his hands and holding it to her belly. "*We* are."

He swallowed hard and realized just how closely

he'd come to losing everything that was worth living for. If he hadn't come to see her, he would have lost Holly. And in losing Holly, he would have lost his child.

And he might never have known.

That thought was enough to terrify him.

But as he looked into gray eyes that held a world of love for him, Parker knew he had dodged that particular bullet—making him the luckiest man alive.

Bending, he planted a kiss on her abdomen, then straightened up and smiled at her. He knew he was looking at a future filled with happiness.

Outside the dressing room, Tommy played the piano, signaling the beginning of the final set of the night.

"I'm so sorry, Parker," Holly said. "I hate to leave you. Especially right now. But I have to get out there."

"Don't be sorry," he said, giving her a quick, hard kiss, feeling the rush of joy race through him. "You're a singer, Holly. I'll never try to change that. I'll always want you to be the woman I fell in love with. The woman I can't live without. And when the show's over, we'll go home. Together."

"Together," she said. "It has a real nice sound to it."

"Sure does," he said, opening the door and stepping back for her to walk past him. Then he dipped his head, and under the noise of the applause, whispered, "Though tomorrow, I'm putting a bed in your dressing room at the jazz café. For those mid-set breaks."

"Mmm…make it a small one," Holly whispered with a smile. "So we'll have to cuddle in close."

"Lady, you've got a deal."

Then he followed her out of the shadows and into the bright glare of the spotlight, knowing that at the end of the night, love would guide them both home.

* * * * *

HOTEL MARCHAND
Four sisters. A family legacy.
And someone is out to destroy it.

A new Harlequin continuity series continues in
November 2006 with
SOME LIKE IT HOT
by Lori Wilde
There's more than cooking going on
in this kitchen....

The kitchen at the Hotel Marchand is hot and
steamy, but it's not the simmering gumbo that's
kicking up the heat. Head chef Robert LeSoeur
and sous-chef Melanie Marchand have been
battling each other since their first day together.
Taking orders and curbing her creative instincts is
tough for an ambitious professional like Melanie.
And the attraction she feels for her boss makes it
even harder. There's only one solution: get rid of
the guy. But Melanie also knows she'd be giving
up the one man she can't afford to lose.

Here's a preview!

As a sous-chef, Melanie was used to the heat. And as the daughter of a Cajun cook, she'd grown up with food preparation running through her veins. She was madly in love with every sultry aspect of the magic that went on in a kitchen.

What she was not accustomed to—and what she was not madly in love with—was having her suggestions shot down without explanation.

She had glanced up at the daily menu posted on the dry erase board by executive chef Robert Le-Soeur and noticed that the innovative creation she'd scribbled down the night before had been slashed through with a bright red marker.

Melanie ground her teeth. Contrariness summoned her, which was odd because she was normally quite happy-go-lucky. Her mood came like a stranger's shadow blocking out the sun on a bright summer day. Something about that exasperating man brought out a whole other side to her and it wasn't pretty.

Fine. If that's the way he wanted it.

This meant war.

Without even a simple FYI, LeSoeur had axed her new specialty dish from the carte du jour. He'd completely dismissed her ideas, making her feel overlooked and insignificant—the way she had often felt growing up as the youngest of four sisters. Charlotte was the smart one, Renee was the pretty one, Sylvie was the funny one and she'd just been the baby.

As she'd gotten older, to compensate for bringing up the rear, Melanie had become the wild one. But her unruly behavior had never stopped her from feeling overshadowed by her more accomplished siblings and coming back home had brought those lurking childhood insecurities back to the forefront.

She hated feeling overshadowed and insecure. It made her want to rebel. And now here was LeSoeur making her feel like a rebellious ten-year-old all over again.

Besides, the turkey was already defrosted and she'd officially had enough of LeSoeur's high-handed ways. It was time for a showdown.

She was making the recipe whether he liked it or

not. He couldn't fire her. Her family owned Chez Remy, an elegant dinner restaurant housed inside the Hotel Marchand, a four-star establishment tucked away on one of the original blocks of the French Quarter.

Purposefully, Melanie squared her shoulders, strode across the cement floor to the stainless-steel commercial refrigerator and with her biceps straining, dragged out the forty-pound turkey. She hauled it over to the prep area and peeled off the plastic wrapper. After removing the giblets, she lubed the turkey up with extra virgin olive oil, all the while ignoring the round-eyed stares of the prep cooks.

The men kept glancing from Melanie to the stroked-out menu item posted near the stove and back again. They recognized mutiny in the offing, but had the good sense not to comment on it. Although Jean-Paul Beaudreau, who had worked for her family since she was a small child, grinned and murmured something in his native Cajun dialect about the sexy appeal of a tempestuous woman.

Humph.

She wasn't tempestuous. She just wanted her voice heard and, damn it, either LeSoeur simply enjoyed provoking her or he needed to be fitted with a high-powered hearing aid. She picked up the oversize bird, now prepped for cooking, and marched it over to the rotisserie.

"It's too big." Robert's voice was a cool caress against her heated ear.

Melanie was startled, but did not look up.

Her insides went soft and weak. Mentally, she steeled herself against the unwanted sensation of sexual attraction by not missing a beat. She kept right on trying to jam the bird into the oven as if Mr. Hot Body himself was not hovering behind her.

He watched her for a few minutes without saying a thing. She could feel his eyes drilling into the back of her head.

A bead of perspiration trickled hotly down her neck.

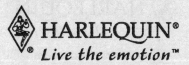

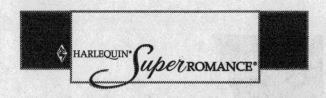

HARLEQUIN® *Super*ROMANCE®

...there's more to the story!

Superromance.
A *big* satisfying read about unforgettable
characters. Each month we offer *six* very different
stories that range from family drama to adventure
and mystery, from highly emotional stories to
romantic comedies—and much more! Stories
about people you'll believe in and care about.
Stories too compelling to put down....

Our authors are among today's *best* romance
writers. You'll find familiar names and talented
newcomers. Many of them are award winners—
and you'll see why!

If you want the biggest and best
in romance fiction, you'll get it
from Superromance!

Emotional, Exciting, Unexpected...

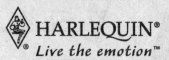

HARLEQUIN®
Live the emotion™

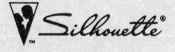

Harlequin Historicals®
Historical Romantic Adventure!

From rugged lawmen and valiant knights to defiant heiresses and spirited frontierswomen, Harlequin Historicals will capture your imagination with their dramatic scope, passion and adventure.

Harlequin Historicals . . . they're too good to miss!

HHDIR104